The Foofoo Tree
and more
Efik Folktales

Edited By Rotimi Ogunjobi

© **2015 Rotimi Ogunjobi**

Illustrations by Ola Tejumola

ISBN: 978-978-53410-2-7

INTRODUCTION TO THE
AFRICAN NIGHT ENTERTAINMENT
SERIES

"....*picture an evening scene in a native village. The sun is nearing the western horizon, seeming to fall like a huge ball behind the distant hills, the air is cool, and a solemn stillness prevails. Even the noisy youths and girls are quiet, and the time for tom-toms, crickets, bull-frogs, and the miscellaneous instruments of man and Nature for the production of the most weird and inharmonious of sounds is not yet. In the compound—the courtyard round which are the family dwellings—the women with their picin (children) on their backs are busy with mortar and pestle making foo-foo (native food from maize). Squatting near the mud walls, naked to the waist, their cloth forming but a covering for the loins, are a number of men smoking short clay pipes and expectorating in a most insanitary manner—a perfect picture of idleness. Naked youngsters stand open-mouthed listening to the conservation of their elders, or amuse themselves at hide-and-seek, marbles, or some other native game.*

The short twilight of the tropics brings all occupations except taking to an end, and of talking there seems to be no end. Here and there someone or other lies down, covers himself entirely with his cloth, and is lost to the world.

A lantern is brought out, and unconsciously and imperceptibly it becomes the centre of dark forms, relieved now and again by rows of beautiful white teeth as the owners indulge in a hearty laugh. At times conversation lags; someone drones a monotonous tune, others smoke in quiet contemplation, while others again follow the example of the dark human mounds scattered about the compound.

Suddenly, "Comrades, listen to a story". At once the men, women, and children press round the speaker, an eager crowd, ready to hear or to tell the tales of their folk...."

                                        -*William H Barker (West African Folktales)*

Where do stories come from?

I asked this question in the preface to a book, Ajantala and other Yoruba Folktales, which I compiled several years ago. For many African children, night time is indeed story time. Children would gathered at the foot of a storyteller, often an elderly person who would entertain them with tales filled with so much drama and passion that they did always appear real , even to listening adults.

But where did those tales come from? Most had indeed been handed down to the storyteller as a child in the same way that he had just done. Sometimes the story would have been so old that the storyteller, not being able to remember how it originally went, would add embellishment of his own crafting, and sometimes in such a proportion that an entirely different tale is consequently produced. I have myself many times, appropriated such creative license while retelling long lost stories to a children audience.

As in every part of the world, the African folktales would generally derive from the daily experience of a people, their environment, their predominant occupations, their aspirations and of course their moral rules. Indeed as an academic discipline, folklore shares methods, and insights with literature, anthropology, art, music, history, linguistics, philosophy, and mythology.

When I say a people, I must add however that the story belongs more to the teller rather than to the community. Depending therefore on the immediate disposition of the storyteller, stories can end up funny , fascinating, ridiculous or thought-provoking, . The constant purpose of the typical African folktale often remains to teach young children important lessons about wholesome values.

One would find from this African Night Entertainment series, that a folktale may be so commonly retold across the continent, that one is no more sure of the origin. As an example, there is much similarity in the story of the bad boy Ajantala, as told by Yoruba folklorist D.O Fagunwa , and the story of the bad boy Kwaku (or Koku) Baboni which existed in Akan folklore more than half a century before Ajantala . One reason for this may have been that African communities and family units used to be very migratory. Indeed, distinct towns and villages in many parts of Africa did not exist until less than three centuries ago. This reason, as well as other factors such as frequent internecine conflicts and slave-raids may have quite assisted the propagation of the folklore of a particular community. Thus, folktales which originated from a specific transient community could eventually become owned by another community, several thousands of miles away, with localized characters.

What have I added to the stories in this series ? In many cases I have tried to preserve the style of the penultimate narrator; rather than making the stories mine. The importance of this is that some folk stories are only interesting if told in a particular way ; otherwise they become so limp and like academic translations. In some cases though, it has been necessary to edit a story primarily for clarity and to simplify obscure and archaic phrases and descriptions. Typically because of the prevalent customs at the time many of these stories were originally generated, one would find instances of ritual murder and demonic manifestation casually thrown in by the narrator ; to the possible distress of the typical prudent reader of these times. In all cases however, I have strived to bring in my personal skill as a storyteller and folklorist, into compiling each priceless volume; I have attempted to give each book the entertainment value it deserves ; I have tried to make each book suitable for preservation in public repositories as the current state of the journey in the storyteller's tale.**Rotimi Ogunjobi**

December 2015

INTRODUCTION
TO THIS VOLUME

The Foo-Foo Tree and more Efik Folktales is a selection of folklore thought to have originated from the Efik people . The Efik are native to South East Nigeria even though they were said to have migrated from the Cameroons.

Originally the economy of the region which they occupy was based on fishing and trading . This aspect of their daily lives as well as the mortal dread of the Ekpe secret society which regularly made and enforced laws, will be seen to have formed the bedrock of their local anecdotes.

Some of the stories in this small volume had been previously retold by a non-native person , to the effect that names are not very accurate in spelling. Indeed some of the names , including those of persons and places, may have actually disappeared from normal usage.

Acknowledgement for some stories in this collection:

Folk Stories from Southern Nigeria, West Africa

By Elphinstone Dayrell

Longman Green and Co. (1910)

CONTENTS

NOTES

AM Book and Team Publishing Limited
1 Olanipekun Street , Ososami Road, Ibadan
Telephone: 08098744910
mail@ambookpublishing.com
www.ambookpublishing.com

THE TORTOISE
AND HIS PRETTY DAUGHTER

There was once a king who was very powerful. He had great influence over the wild beasts and animals. Now the tortoise was looked upon as the wisest of all beasts and men. This king had a son named Ekpenyong to whom he gave fifty young girls as wives, but the prince did not like any of them. The king was very angry at this and made a law that if any man had a daughter who was more beautiful than the prince's wives, and who found favor in his son's eyes, the girl and her parents should be killed.

About this time, the tortoise and his wife had a daughter who was very beautiful. The mother thought it was not safe to keep such a fine child as the prince might fall in love with her, so she told her husband that their daughter should be killed and thrown away into the bush. The tortoise, however, was unwilling, and hid her until she was three years old.

One day, when the tortoise and his wife were away on their farm, the king's son was hunting near their house and saw a bird perched on the top of the fence round the house. The bird was watching the little girl and was so captivated by her beauty that it did

13

not notice the prince coming. The prince shot the bird with his bow and arrow and it dropped inside the fence, so the prince sent his servant to fetch it. While the servant was looking for the bird, he came across the little girl and was so struck with her beauty that he immediately returned to his master and told him what he had seen.

The prince then broke down the fence and found the child, and fell in love with her at once. He stayed and talked with her for a long time, until at last she agreed to become his wife. He then went home, but concealed from his father the fact that he had fallen in love with the beautiful daughter of the tortoise. The next morning, he sent for the treasurer and got sixty pieces of cloth and three hundred rods, and sent them to the tortoise. Then in the early afternoon, he went to the tortoise's house and told him that he wished to marry his daughter.

The tortoise saw at once that what he feared had come to pass and that his life was in danger, so he told the prince that if the king knew the prince's intention, he would kill him, his wife and daughter, and also the prince. The prince replied that he would have to be killed first before he allowed the tortoise and his wife and daughter to be killed.

Eventually, after much argument, the tortoise consented and agreed to hand his daughter to the prince as his wife when she became old enough. Then the prince went home and told his mother what he had done. She was in great distress at the thought that she would lose her son of whom she was very proud, as she knew that when the king heard of his son's disobedience he would kill him. However, although the queen knew how angry her husband would be, she wanted her son to marry the girl he had fallen in love with, so she went to the tortoise and gave him some money, clothes, yams and palm-oil as further dowry on her son's behalf in order that the tortoise should not give his daughter to another man.

For the next five years, the prince was constantly with the tortoise's daughter whose name was Edet; and when she was about to be put in the fattening house, the prince told his father that he was going to take Edet as his wife. On hearing this, the king was very angry and sent word all round his kingdom that all the people should come on a certain day to the market place to hear the matter. On the appointed day, the market place was quite full of people and the stones belonging to the king and queen were placed in the middle.

When the king and queen arrived, the people stood up and greeted them and sat down on their stones. The king then told his attendants to bring the girl, Edet, before him. The king was quite astonished at her beauty when he saw her. He then told the people that he had sent for them to tell them that he was angry with his son for disobeying him and taking Edet as his wife without his knowledge. But that now that he had seen her himself, he had to admit that she was very beautiful and that his son had made a good choice and he would therefore forgive his son.

The people also agreed that she was very fine and quite worthy of being the prince's wife and begged the king to cancel the law he had made altogether, and the king agreed. The law was made under the *Ekpe* law so he sent for eight *Ekpes* and told them that the order was cancelled throughout his kingdom, and that for the future no one who had a daughter more beautiful than the prince's wives would be killed. He gave the *Ekpes* palm wine and money to remove the law, and sent them away. Then he declared that the tortoise's daughter, Edet, should marry his son, and he made them marry the same day.

A great feast was given which lasted for fifty days, and the king killed five cows and gave all the people plenty of *foo-foo* and palm-oil stew, and placed a large number of pots of palm wine in the streets for the people to drink as they liked. The women brought a big ceremony to the king's compound and there was singing and dancing day and night during the whole time. The prince and his companions also danced and made merry in the market square.

When the feast was over, the king gave half of his kingdom to the tortoise to rule over, and three hundred slaves to work on his farm. The prince also gave his father-in-law two hundred women and one hundred girls to work for him, so the tortoise became one of the richest men in the kingdom. The prince and his wife lived together for many years until the king died and the prince ruled in his place.

THE CRAFTY HUNTER

Many years ago, there was a Calabar hunter called Effiong, who lived in the bush, killed a great number of animals, and made much money. Everyone in the country knew him, and one of his best friends was a man called Okon, who lived near him. But Effiong was very extravagant and spent much money in eating and drinking with everyone until at last he became quite poor, so he had to go out hunting again. But now his good luck seemed to have deserted him, for although he worked hard and hunted day and night, he could not succeed in killing anything. One day, as he was very hungry, he went to his friend, Okon, and borrowed two hundred rods from him. He told him to come to his house on a certain day to get his money and to bring his loaded gun with him.

Sometime before this, Effiong had made friends with a leopard and a bush cat whom he had met in the forest whilst on one of his hunting expeditions. He had also made friends with a goat and a rooster at a farm where he had stayed for the night. But though Effiong had borrowed money from Okon, he could not think of how he was to repay it on the day he had promised. At last, however, he

18

thought of a plan and on the next day he went to his friend, the leopard, and asked him to lend him two hundred rods, promising to return the amount to him on the same day as he had promised to pay Okon. He also told the leopard that if he were absent when he came for his money, he could kill anything he saw in the house and eat it. The leopard was then to wait until the hunter arrived when he would pay him the money; and to this the leopard agreed.

The hunter then went to his friend, the goat, and borrowed two hundred rods from him in the same way. Effiong also went to his friends, the bush cat and the rooster, and borrowed two hundred rods from each of them on the same conditions. He also told each of them that if he were absent when they arrived, they could kill and eat anything they found around his house.

When the appointed day arrived, the hunter spread some corn on the ground and then went away and left the house deserted. Very early in the morning, soon after the rooster had begun to crow, he remembered what the hunter had told him and walked over to the hunter's house but found no one there. On looking round, however, he saw some corn on the ground and being hungry, he commenced to eat. About this time the bush cat also arrived, and not finding the hunter at home, he looked about and saw the rooster who was busy picking up the grains of corn. So the bush cat went up very softly behind, pounced on the rooster, killed him at once and began to eat him. By this time the goat had come for his money too, but not finding his friend, he walked about until he came upon the bush cat who was so intent upon his meal of the rooster that he did not notice the goat approaching. And the goat, being in a rather bad temper for not getting his money, charged at the bush cat and knocked him over, butting him with his horns. The bush cat did not like this at all but as he was not big enough to fight the goat, he picked up the remains of the rooster and ran off with it to the bush. Thus he lost his money as he did not await the arrival of the hunter.

The goat was then left master of the situation and started bleating. This noise attracted the attention of the leopard who was on his way to receive his money from Effiong. As he got nearer, the smell of goat became very strong and being hungry for he had not eaten anything for some time, he approached the goat very carefully. Not seeing anyone about, he stalked the goat and got nearer until he was within springing distance. The goat, in the meantime, was grazing quietly, quite unsuspicious of any danger as he was in his friend, the hunter's compound. Now and then he would say *"meehehe!"* But most of the time he was busy eating the young grass and picking up the leaves which had fallen from a tree of which he was very fond. Suddenly, the leopard leapt at the goat and with one crunch at the neck brought him down. The goat was dead immediately and the leopard started on his meal.

It was now about eight o'clock in the morning and Okon, the hunter's friend, having had his early morning meal, went out with his gun to receive payment of the two hundred rods he had lent to the hunter. When he got close to the house, he heard a crunching sound and being a hunter himself, he approached very cautiously. Looking over the fence, he saw the leopard only a few yards off, busily engaged eating the goat. He took careful aim at the leopard and fired and the leopard rolled over dead. The death of the leopard meant that four of the hunter's creditors were now disposed of: as the bush cat had killed the rooster, the goat had driven the bush cat away, and the goat had been killed by the leopard who had just been killed by Okon.

This meant a saving of eight hundred rods to Effiong but he was not content with this. Immediately he heard the report of the gun, he ran out from where he had been hiding and found the leopard lying dead with Okon standing over it. Then in very strong language, Effiong began to scold his friend and asked him why he had killed his old friend, the leopard. He said nothing would satisfy him than to report the whole matter to the king who would no doubt deal with him as he thought fit. Okon was frightened and pleaded with Effiong not to say anything more about the matter as the king would be angry but the hunter was adamant and refused to listen to him. And at last Okon said, "If you will allow the whole thing to drop and will say no more about it, I will give you the two hundred rods you borrowed from me." This was just what Effiong wanted, but still he did not give in at once. Eventually, he agreed and told Okon to go and that he would bury the body of his friend, the leopard.

Immediately Okon had gone, instead of burying the body, Effiong dragged it inside the house and skinned it very carefully. The skin he put out to dry in the sun and covered it with wood ash, and the body he ate. When the skin was well dried, he took it to a distant market where he sold it for much money.

And now, whenever a bush cat sees a rooster he always kills it, and does so by right, as he takes the rooster in part payment of the two hundred rods which the hunter never paid him.

THE FOO-FOO TREE

Effiong Duke was an ancient king of Calabar. He was a peaceful man, and did not like war. He had a wonderful drum which when beaten, always provided a great deal of good foods and drinks. So whenever any country declared war against him, he would call all his enemies together and beat his drum. And to the surprise of everyone, instead of fighting, the people found tables spread with all sorts of dishes: fish, *foo-foo*, palm-oil soup, cooked yams and okras, and plenty palm wine for everybody. In this way, he kept all the country quiet and sent his enemies away with full stomachs and quite contented. There was only one drawback to possessing the drum, and that was if the owner of the drum walked over any stick on the road or stepped over a fallen tree, all the food would immediately go bad and three hundred *Ekpe* men would appear with sticks and whips and beat the owner of the drum and all the invited guests very severely.

Effiong Duke was a rich man. He had many farms and hundreds of slaves, a large store of palm kernels on the beach and many casks of palm-oil. He also had fifty wives and many children.

23

The wives were all fine women and healthy. They were also good mothers and all of them had many children, which was good for the king's house.

Every few months, the king issued invitations to all his subjects to come to a big feast. Even the wild animals were invited; the elephants, hippopotami, leopards, bush cows, and antelopes used to come. In those days they were friendly with man and when they were at the feast they did not kill one another. All the people and the animals as well were envious of the king's drum and wanted to own it but the king would not part with it.

One morning, Edem, one of the king's wives, took her little daughter down to the spring to wash her as she was covered with scabies, which are bad sores all over the body. The tortoise happened to be up a palm tree just over the spring, cutting nuts for his midday meal and one of the nuts fell to the ground just in front of the child. The little girl, seeing the good food, cried for it and the mother not knowing any better, picked up the palm nut and gave it to her daughter.

Immediately the tortoise saw this, he climbed down the tree and asked the woman where his palm nut was. She replied that she had given it to her child to eat. Then the tortoise who very much wanted the king's drum, thought he would make a lot of trouble over this and force the king to give him the drum, so he said to the mother of the child, "I am a poor man, and I climbed the tree to get food for myself and my family, then you took my palm nut and gave it to your child. I shall tell the whole matter to the king and see what he has to say when he hears that one of his wives has stolen my food." As everyone knew, this was a very serious crime according to native custom.

Edem then said to the tortoise, "I saw your palm nut lying on the ground and thinking it had fallen from the tree, I gave it to my little girl to eat. I did not steal it. My husband, the king, is a rich man, and if you have any complaint to make against me or my child, I will take you before him." So when she had finished washing her daughter at the spring, she took the tortoise to her husband and told him what had taken place. The king then asked the tortoise what he would accept as compensation for the loss of his palm nut. He offered him money, cloth, kernels or palm-oil, all of which the tortoise refused one after the other.

The king then said to the tortoise, "What will you take? You may have anything you like." And the tortoise immediately pointed to the king's drum and said that it was the only thing he wanted. In order to get rid of the tortoise, the king said, "Very well, take the drum." But he never told the tortoise about the bad things that would happen to him if he stepped over a fallen tree or walked over a stick on the road.

The tortoise was very glad and he carried the drum home in triumph to his wife, and said, "I am now a rich man, and shall do no more work. Whenever I want food, all I have to do is to beat this drum, and food will immediately be brought to me and a lot to drink."

His wife and children were very pleased when they heard this and asked the tortoise to get food at once as they were all hungry. The tortoise was very pleased to do this as he wished to show off his newly acquired wealth and was also hungry himself. He beat the drum in the same way as he had seen the king do when he wanted something to eat. Immediately, so much food appeared and they all sat down and made a great feast. The tortoise did this for three days and everything went well. All his children got fat because they had as much as they could possibly eat.

The tortoise was very proud of his drum and in order to display his riches, he sent invitations to the king and all the people and animals to come to a feast. When the people received their invitations, they laughed and very few attended the feast as they knew the tortoise was very poor. But the king, knowing about the drum, came. The tortoise beat the drum and food was brought as usual in great quantity and all the people sat down and enjoyed their meal. They were much astonished that the poor tortoise could entertain so many people and told all their friends what fine dishes had been placed before them, and that they had never had a better dinner. The people who had not gone were very sorry when they heard this, as a good feast at somebody else's expense is not provided every day.

After the feast, all the people looked upon the tortoise as one of the richest men in the kingdom and he was very much respected as a result. No one, except the king, could understand how the poor tortoise could suddenly entertain so lavishly, but they all made up their minds that if the tortoise ever gave another feast, they would not refuse again.

When the tortoise had been in possession of the drum for a few weeks, he became lazy and did no work but went about the country boasting of his riches, and took to drinking too much. One day, after he had been drinking a lot of palm wine at a distant farm, he started home carrying his drum but having had too much to drink, he did not notice a stick in the path. He walked over the stick and of

course, the *Juju* was broken at once. But he did not know this, as nothing happened at the time. Eventually, he arrived at his house very tired and still not very well from having drunk too much. He threw the drum into a corner and went to sleep.

He woke up in the morning very hungry and his wife and children were calling out for food too. The tortoise beat the drum but instead of food being brought, the house was filled with *Ekpe* men who beat the tortoise, his wife and children badly. At this the tortoise was very angry and said to himself, "I asked everyone to a feast, but only a few came and they had so much to eat and drink. Now when I want food for myself and my family, the *Ekpes* come and beat me. Well, I will let the other people share the same fate as I do not see why I and my family alone should be beaten when I have given a feast to all people." He therefore sent out invitations to all the men and animals to come to a big lunch the next day at three o'clock in the afternoon.

This time, many people came as they did not wish to lose the chance of a free meal a second time. Even the sick men, the lame and the blind got their friends to lead them to the feast. When they had all arrived, with the exception of the king and his wives who sent excuses, the tortoise beat his drum as usual and then quickly hid himself under a bench where he could not be seen. He had sent his wife and children away before the feast as he knew what would surely happen. As he beat the drum, three hundred *Ekpe* men appeared with whips and started flogging all the guests. They could not escape as the doors had been fastened. The beating went on for two hours, and the people were so badly punished that many of them had to be carried home on the backs of their friends. The leopard was the only one who escaped as he saw the *Ekpe* men arrive and knew that things were likely to be unpleasant.

When the tortoise was satisfied with the beating the people had received, he crept to the door and opened it and the people ran away. The tortoise then tapped the drum in a certain way and all the *Ekpe* men vanished. The people who had been beaten were so angry and made so much trouble with the tortoise that he made up his mind to return the drum to the king the next day. So in the morning, the tortoise went to the king and brought the drum with him. He told the king that he was not satisfied with the drum and wished to exchange it for something else. He did not mind so much what the king gave him, so long as he got full value for the drum. He was quite willing to accept a certain number of slaves, a few farms or their equivalent in cloth or rods.

The king, however, refused to do this. But as he was sorry for the tortoise, he decided to present him with a magic *foo-foo* tree which would provide the tortoise and his family with food if he kept a certain condition. To this, the tortoise gladly consented. Now this *foo-foo* tree only bore fruit once a year, but every day it dropped *foo-foo* and soup on the ground. And the condition was that the owner should gather sufficient food for the day, once, and not return for more. The tortoise, when he had thanked the king for his generosity, went home to his wife and told her to bring her calabashes to the tree. She did so and they gathered a great deal of *foo-foo* and soup quite sufficient for the whole family for that day and went back to their house very happy.

That night, they all feasted and enjoyed themselves. But one of the tortoise's sons, who was very greedy, thought to himself, "I wonder where my father gets all this good food from. I must ask him." So in the morning he said to his father, "Tell me, from where do you get all this *foo-foo* and soup?" But his father refused to tell him because the tortoise's wife who was also a cunning woman said, "If we let our children know the secret of the *foo-foo* tree, someday when they are hungry after we have got our daily supply, one of them may go to the tree and gather more, which will break the *Juju*."

But the covetous son, being determined to get food for himself, decided to track his father to the place where he got the food. This was somewhat difficult to do as the tortoise always went out alone and took the greatest care to prevent anyone from following him. However, the boy soon thought of a plan, and got a calabash with a long neck and a hole in the end. He filled the calabash with wood ashes which he obtained from the fire, and then got the bag which his father always carried on his back when he went out to get food. He made a small hole in the bottom of the bag and inserted the calabash with the neck downwards, so that when his father walked to the *foo-foo* tree he would leave a small trail of wood ashes behind him.

The next day, the tortoise slung his bag over his back as usual and set out to get the daily supply of food. His greedy son followed the trail of the wood ashes, making sure he hid himself and not let his father sense that he was being followed. At last the tortoise arrived at the tree, placed his calabashes on the ground and collected the food for the day, the boy watching him from a distance. When his father finished and left for home, the boy also returned and said nothing to his parents. He had a good meal and went to bed. After he was certain his parents were deeply asleep, he got some of his brothers to go to the *foo-foo* tree with him. They collected *foo-foo* and soup even more than the tortoise did and so broke the *Juju*.

At daylight, the tortoise went to the tree as usual but he could not find it as during the night, the whole bush had grown up and the *foo-foo* tree was hidden from sight. There was nothing to be seen but a dense mass of prickly *tie-tie* palm. The tortoise knew at once that someone had broken the *Juju* and had gathered *foo-foo* from the tree twice in the same day. He returned very sadly to his house and told his wife. He then called all his family together and told them what had happened, and asked them who had done this evil thing. They all denied having had anything to do with the tree. In despair, the tortoise brought all his family to the place where the *foo-foo* tree had been but which was now all prickly *tie-tie* palm, and said, "My dear wife and children, I have done all that I can for you but you have broken my *Juju*; you must therefore for the future live on the *tie-tie* palm." So they made their home underneath the prickly tree, and from that day you will always find tortoises living under the prickly *tie-tie* palm as they have nowhere else to go to for food.

THE DISOBEDIENT DAUGHTER WHO MARRIED A SKULL

Effiong Edem was a native of Cobham Town. He had a very fine daughter whose name was Afiong. All the young men in the country wanted to marry her because of her beauty but in spite of repeated pleadings from her parents, she refused all offers of marriage. She was very vain and said she would only marry the best looking man in the country, who would have to be young, strong, and capable of loving her properly. Most of the men her parents wanted her to marry, although rich, were old men and ugly. So the girl continued to disobey her parents, at which they were very sad.

The skull who lived in the spirit land heard of the beauty of this Calabar virgin, and thought he would like to marry her. He went to his friends and borrowed different parts of the body from them, all of the best. From one he got a good head, another lent him a body, a third gave him strong arms, and a fourth lent him a fine pair of legs. At last he was complete, and was a very perfect specimen of manhood. He then left the spirit land and went to Cobham market where he saw Afiong and admired her very much.

Afiong heard that a very fine man who was better-looking than any of the natives had been seen in the market, so she went to the market and saw the skull in his borrowed beauty. She fell in love with him and invited him to her house. The skull was delighted and went home with her. On his arrival, he was introduced by the girl to her parents and immediately asked their consent to marry their daughter. At first they refused, as they did not wish her to marry a stranger, but they eventually agreed.

The skull lived with Afiong for two days in her parents' house, and then said he wished to take his wife back to his country which was far off. To this the girl readily agreed as he was such a fine man, but her parents tried to persuade her not to go. But being very headstrong, she made up her mind to go and they started off together. After they had been gone a few days, the father consulted his *Juju* man, who by casting lots discovered that his daughter's husband belonged to the spirit land and that she would surely be killed. They therefore all mourned her as dead.

After walking for several days, Afiong and the skull crossed the border between the spirit land and the human country. As they set foot in the spirit land, one man came to the skull and demanded his legs, then another his head, and the next his body, and so on, until in a few minutes the skull was left by itself in all its natural ugliness. At this the girl was very frightened and wanted to return home, but the skull would not allow this and ordered her to go with him.

When they arrived at the skull's house, they found his mother who was a very old woman quite incapable of doing any work and who could only creep about. Afiong tried her best to help her. She cooked for her and brought water and firewood for the old woman. The old creature was very grateful for these attentions and soon became quite fond of Afiong.

One day, the old woman told Afiong that she was very sorry for her. She told her that all the people in the spirit land were cannibals and when they heard there was a human being in their country, they would come down to kill and eat her. But as Afiong had looked after the old woman so well, the skull's mother hid Afiong and promised she would send her back to her country as soon as possible, on the condition that she began to obey her parents. This Afiong readily consented to do.

Then the old woman sent for the spider who was a very clever hairdresser and made him dress Afiong's hair in the latest fashion. She also presented her with anklets and other things on account of her kindness. She then made a *Juju* and called the winds to come and take

Afiong away to her home. At first, a violent tornado came with thunder, lightning and rain, but the skull's mother sent him away as unsuitable. The next wind to come was a gentle breeze, so she told the breeze to carry Afiong to her mother's house, and said good-bye to her. Very soon afterwards, the breeze deposited Afiong outside her home and left her there.

Afiong's parents were very glad when they saw their daughter, as they had for some months given her up as dead. The father spread soft animals' skins on the ground from where his daughter was standing all the way to the house, so that her feet should not be soiled. Afiong then walked to the house and her father called all the young girls who were Afiong's friends to come and dance, and the feasting and dancing was kept up for eight days and nights.

When the rejoicing was over, the father reported what had happened to the head chief of the town. The chief then passed a law that parents should never allow their daughters to marry strangers who came from a far country. Then the father told Afiong to marry a friend of his and she willingly consented and lived with him for many years and had many children.

THE KING WHO MARRIED THE ROOSTER'S DAUGHTER

King Effiom of Duke Town, Calabar, was very fond of pretty maidens and whenever he heard of a girl who was unusually good-looking, he always sent for her and if she took his fancy, he made her one of his wives. This he could afford to do as he was a rich man and could pay any dowry which the parents asked, most of his money having been made by buying and selling slaves.

Effiom had two hundred and fifty wives, but he was never content and wanted to have all the finest women in the land. Some of the king's friends who were always on the look-out for pretty girls, told Effiom that the rooster's daughter, called Adia Unen, was a lovely girl, and far more beautiful than any of the king's wives. Immediately the king heard this, he sent for the rooster and told him he intended to marry his daughter. The rooster, being a poor man, could not resist the order of the king, so he brought his daughter who was very good-looking to the king and this pleased him immensely. When the king had paid the rooster a dowry of six casks of palm-oil, the cock told Effiom that he must not forget that Adia Unen had the natural instincts of a hen, and that he should not blame her if she picked up corn whenever she saw it. The king replied that he did not mind what she ate so long as he owned her.

The king then took Adia Unen as his wife and liked her so much that he neglected all his other wives. He lived fully with her as she suited him well and pleased him more than any of his other wives. She also amused the king, played with him and was so friendly with him in so many different ways that he could not live without her. He always had her with him, to the exclusion of his former favorites whom he would not even speak to or notice in any way.

This so enraged the neglected wives that they met together, and although they all hated one another, they agreed that they hated the rooster's daughter more as the king no longer had time for anyone of them since Adia Unen came. Formerly, though the king had his favorites, he used to give them due attention, especially when they pleased him. In their opinion, that was better than being excluded from his presence and all his affections concentrated on one girl who received all his love and embraces. They were very angry and determined, if possible, to disgrace Adia Unen.

After much discussion, one of the wives who was the last favorite and whom the arrival of the rooster's daughter had displaced, said, "This girl, whom we all hate, is after all only a rooster's daughter and we can easily disgrace her before the king. I heard her father tell the king that she could not resist corn no matter how it was thrown about."

Very shortly after the king's wives had determined to try to disgrace Adia Unen, all the people of the country came to pay homage to the king. This was done three times a year, with the people bringing yams, fowls, goats and new corn as presents, and the king entertained them with a feast of *foo-foo*, palm-oil chop, and *tombo*. A big dance was also held which was usually kept up for several days and nights. Early in the morning, the king's head wife told her servant to wash one head of corn and when all the people were present she was to bring it in a calabash and throw it on the ground and then walk away. The corn was to be thrown in front of Adia Unen, so that all the people and chiefs could see.

About ten o'clock when all the chiefs and people had assembled and the king had taken his seat on his big wooden chair, the servant girl came and threw the corn on the ground as she had been ordered. Immediately she did this, Adia Unen started towards the corn, picked it up, and began to eat. At this all the people laughed and the king was very angry and ashamed. The king's wives and many people said that they thought the king's finest wife would have learnt better manners than to pick up corn which had been thrown away as refuse. Others said: "What can you expect from a rooster's daughter? She should not be blamed for obeying her natural instincts." But the king was so vexed that he told one of his servants to pack up Adia Unen's things and take them to her father's house. This was done and Aida Unen returned to her parents.

That night, the king's third wife, who was a friend of Adia Unen, talked the whole matter over with the king, and explained to him that it was entirely owing to the jealousy of his head wife that Adia Unen was disgraced. She told him that the whole thing had been arranged beforehand in order that the king should get rid of Adia Unen of whom all the other wives were jealous. The king was very angry when he heard this and he made up his mind to send the jealous woman back to her parents empty-handed, without her clothes and presents. When she arrived at her father's house, her parents refused to take her in. She had been given as a wife to the king and whenever the parents wanted anything, they always got it at the palace. It was therefore a great loss to them. She was thus turned into the streets and walked about very miserable, and after a time died very poor and starving.

The king was so sad at having been compelled to send his favorite wife, Adia Unen, away that he died the following year. And when the people saw that their king had died of a broken heart, they passed a law that for the future no one should marry any bird or animal.

THE WOMAN, THE APE, AND THE CHILD

Okon Archibong was one of King Archibong's slaves and he lived on a farm near Calabar. He was a hunter and used to kill bush buck and other kinds of antelopes and many monkeys. He used to spread the skins in the sun and when they were properly dried, he would sell them in the market. The monkey skins were used for making drums and the antelope skins were used for sitting mats. He also sold the flesh after it had been well smoked over a wood fire, though he did not make much money from it.

Okon Archibong married a slave woman of Duke's house named Nkoyo. He paid a small dowry to the Dukes, took his wife home to his farm and in the dry season she had a son. About four months after the birth of the child, Nkoyo took him to the farm while her husband was away hunting. She placed the little boy under a shady tree and was clearing the ground for the yams which would be planted about two months before the rains.

Every day while Nkoyo worked, a big ape came from the forest to play with the little boy. He would hold him in his arms and carry him up a tree and when Nkoyo had finished her work, he would bring the baby back to her. There was a hunter named Edem Effiong who had for a long time been in love with Nkoyo and had made advances to her, but she would have nothing to do with him as she was very fond of her husband. When she had her little child, Effiong Edem was very jealous and meeting her one day on the farm without her baby, he asked, "Where is your baby?" And she replied that a big ape had taken it up a tree and was looking after it for her. When Effiong Edem saw that the ape was a big one, he made up his mind to tell Nkoyo's husband.

The very next day, he told Okon Archibong that he had seen his wife in the forest with a big ape. At first Okon would not believe this but the hunter told him to come with him so he could see it with his own eyes. Okon Archibong therefore made up his mind to kill the ape. The next day, he went with the hunter to the farm and saw the ape up a tree playing with his son. He took very careful aim and shot the ape, but it did not die. It was so angry and its strength was so great that it tore the child limb from limb and threw it to the ground. This so enraged Okon Archibong that seeing his wife standing near, he shot her also. He then ran home and told King Archibong what had taken place.

This king was very brave and fond of fighting so as he knew that King Duke would be certain to make war on him, he immediately called in all his fighting men. When he was quite prepared, he sent a messenger to tell King Duke what had happened. Duke was very angry and sent the messenger back to King Archibong to say that he must send the hunter to him so that he could kill him in any way he pleased. This, Archibong refused to do, and said he would rather fight. Duke then got his men together and both sides met and fought in the market square. Thirty men were killed of Duke's men and twenty were killed on Archibong's side; there were also many wounded.

On the whole, King Archibong had the best of the fighting and drove King Duke back. When the fighting was at its hottest, the other chiefs sent out all the *Ekpe* men with drums and stopped the fight, and the next day the matter was tried in *Ekpe* house. King Archibong was found guilty and was ordered to pay six thousand rods to King Duke. He refused to pay this amount to Duke and said he would rather go on fighting. But as the *Ekpes* had decided the case, he said he did not mind paying the six thousand rods to the town.

They were about to commence fighting again when the whole country rose up and said it was enough. Archibong then told Duke that the woman's death was not really the fault of his slave, Okon Archibong, but of Effiong Edem, who made the false report. When

Duke heard this, he agreed to leave the whole matter to the chiefs to decide, and Effiong Edem was called to take his place on the stone. He was tried and found guilty and two *Ekpes* came out armed with cutting whips and gave him two hundred lashes on his bare back, and then cut off his head and sent it to Duke who placed it before his *Juju*.

From that time to the present, all apes and monkeys have been frightened of human beings, and even of little children. The *Ekpes* also passed a law that a chief should not allow his men slaves to marry women slaves of another house as it would probably lead to fighting.

WHY THE BAT IS ASHAMED TO BE SEEN IN THE DAYTIME

There was once an old mother sheep who had seven lambs. One day, the bat who was about to make a visit to his father-in-law who lived a long day's walk away, went to the old sheep and asked her to lend him one of her young lambs to carry his load for him. At first the mother sheep refused, but as the young lamb was anxious to travel and see something of the world and begged to be allowed to go, she reluctantly consented. So in the morning at daylight, the bat and the lamb set off together with the lamb carrying the bat's drinking-horn. When they reached halfway, the bat told the lamb to leave the horn underneath a bamboo tree.

Immediately they arrived at the house, he sent the lamb back to get the horn. When the lamb had gone, the bat's father-in-law brought him food and the bat ate it all, leaving nothing for the lamb. When the lamb returned, the bat said to him, "Hullo! You have arrived at last I see, but you are too late for food; it is all finished." He then sent the lamb back to the tree with the horn, and when the lamb returned again it was late, and he went to bed without supper. The next day, just before it was time for food, the bat sent the lamb off again for the drinking-horn and when the food arrived, the bat who was very greedy, ate it all up a second time. This mean behavior on the part of the bat went on for four days until at last the lamb became quite thin and weak. The bat decided to return home the next day, and it was all the lamb could do to carry his load.

When he got home to his mother, the lamb complained bitterly of the treatment he had received from the bat and kept screeching all night, complaining of pains in his inside. The old mother sheep, who was very fond of her children, determined to revenge on the bat for the cruel way he had starved her lamb. She therefore decided to consult the tortoise who although very poor, was considered by all people to be the wisest of all animals. When the old sheep had told the whole story to the tortoise, he considered for some time and then told the sheep to leave the matter entirely to him, that he would take ample revenge on the bat for his cruel treatment of her son.

Very soon after this, the bat decided again to go and see his father-in-law, so he went to the mother sheep and asked her for one of her sons to carry his load as before. The tortoise, who happened to be present, told the bat that he was going in that direction and would cheerfully carry his load for him. They set out on their journey the following day and when they arrived at the half-way resting place, the bat used the same trick that he had used on the previous occasion. He told the tortoise to hide his drinking horn under the same tree as the lamb had hidden it before. This the tortoise did but when the bat was not looking, he picked up the drinking horn and hid it in his bag. When they arrived at the house, the tortoise hung the horn out of sight in the backyard, and then sat down in the house.

Just before it was time for food, the bat sent the tortoise to get the drinking horn. The tortoise went outside into the yard and waited until he heard that the beating of the boiled yams into *foo-foo* had finished. He then went into the house and gave the drinking horn to the bat who was so surprised and angry that when the food was passed, he refused to eat any of it and the tortoise ate it all. This went on for four days until at last the bat became as thin as the poor little lamb had been on the previous occasion. At last, the bat could no longer stand the pains inside him and he secretly told his mother-in-law to bring him food when the tortoise was not looking. He said, "I am now going to sleep a little but you can wake me up when the food is ready."

The tortoise, who had been listening all the time, having hidden in a corner of the room, waited until the bat was fast asleep and then carried him very gently into the next room and placed him on his own bed. He then very softly and quietly took off the bat's cloth and covered himself in it and lay down where the bat had been. Very soon, the bat's mother-in-law brought the food and placed it next to where the bat was supposed to be sleeping. She pulled his cloth to wake him and went away. The tortoise then got up and ate all the food. And when he had finished, he carried the bat back again to his room, took some of the palm-oil and *foo-foo* and placed it inside the bat's lips while he was asleep, then the tortoise went to sleep.

In the morning when he woke up, the bat was hungrier than ever and in a very bad temper. He sought out his mother-in-law and started scolding her, asking her why she had not brought his food as he had told her to do. She replied she had brought his food and that he had eaten it but the bat denied this and accused the tortoise of having eaten the food. The woman then said she would call the people in to decide the matter. But the tortoise slipped out first and told the people that the best way to find out who had eaten the food was to make both the bat and himself rinse their mouths out with clean water into a basin. They agreed to do this, so the tortoise got the tooth-stick which he always used and having cleaned his teeth properly, washed his mouth out and returned to the house.

When all the people had arrived, the woman told them how the bat had abused her. And as he still maintained stoutly that he had had no food for five days, the people said that both he and the tortoise should wash their mouths out with clean water into two clean calabashes. This was done and at once it could clearly be seen that the bat had been eating as there were on the water, distinct traces of the palm-oil and *foo-foo* which the tortoise had put inside the bat's lips. The people decided against the bat when they saw this, and he was so ashamed that he ran away then and there. Ever since, he has always hidden himself in the bush during the daytime so that no one could see him and only comes out at night to get his food.

The next day, the tortoise returned to the mother sheep and told her what he had done and that the bat was forever disgraced. The old sheep praised him very much and told all her friends. This greatly increased the reputation of the tortoise for wisdom throughout the whole country.

WHY THE BUSH COW AND
THE ELEPHANT ARE NOT FRIENDS

> **Comment [kC]:** I think the name of the chief and the town should be mentioned.

The bush cow and the elephant were always bad friends. And as they could not settle their disputes between themselves, they agreed to let the head chief decide. The cause of their enmity was that the elephant was always boasting about his strength to all his friends, which made the bush cow ashamed as he was a good fighter and feared no man or animal. When the matter was referred to the head chief, he decided that the best way to settle the dispute was for the elephant and bush cow to meet and fight each other in a large open space. He decided that the fight should take place in the market place on the next market day when all the country people could witness the battle.

On the agreed market day, the bush cow went out in the early morning, took up his position some distance from the town on the main road to the market, and started bellowing and tearing up the ground. As the people passed, he asked them whether they had seen anything of the "*Big, Big One,*" which was the name of the elephant. A bush buck, who happened to be passing, replied, "I am only a small antelope, and I am on my way to the market. How should I know anything of the movements of the *Big, Big One?*" The bush cow then allowed him to pass.

After a little time, the bush cow heard the elephant trumpeting and could hear him as he came nearer, breaking down trees and trampling down small bushes. When the elephant came near the bush cow, they both charged at each other and a memorable fight commenced in which a lot of damage was done to the surrounding farms, and many of the people were afraid to go to the market and returned to their houses.

At last, the monkey, who had been watching the fight from a distance whilst he was jumping from branch to branch high up in the trees, thought he would report what he had seen to the head chief. Although he forgot several times what it was he wanted to do (which is a little way monkeys have), he eventually reached the chief's house and jumped on the roof where he caught and ate a spider. He then climbed to the ground again and began to play with a small stick. But he very soon got tired of this and picking up a stone, he rubbed it backward and forward on the ground in an aimless sort of way while he looked in the opposite direction.

His attention was soon attracted to a large praying mantis which had fluttered into the house, making much noise with its wings.

When it settled, it immediately assumed its usual prayerful posture. The monkey, after carefully stalking the insect, seized the mantis and deliberately pulled the legs off one after the other. He ate the body and sat down with his head on one side, looking very wise but in reality thinking of nothing.

Just then the chief caught sight of the monkey scratching himself and shouted out in a loud voice, "Ha, monkey, is that you? What do you want here?"

At the chief's voice, the monkey jumped up, startled and started chattering like a parrot. After a time he replied very nervously, "Oh yes, of course! Yes, I came to see you." Then he said to himself, "I wonder what on earth it was I came to tell the chief?" But it was no use, everything had gone out of his head.

The chief told the monkey he might take one of the ripe plantains hanging up in the veranda. The monkey did not wait to be told twice as he was very fond of plantains. He soon tore off the skin and holding the plantain in both hands, took bite after bite from the end of it, looking at it carefully after each bite.

Then the chief remarked that the elephant and the bush cow ought to have arrived by that time as they were going to have a great fight. Immediately the monkey heard this, he remembered what it was he wanted to tell the chief. Having swallowed the piece of plantain he had placed in the side of his cheek, he said, "Ah! That reminds me." And then after much chattering and making all sorts of funny grimaces, he finally told the chief that the elephant and bush cow were fighting in the bush on the main road leading to the market and had thus stopped most of the people coming in.

When the chief heard this, he was angry. He called for his bow and poisoned arrows and went to the scene of the fight. He shot both the elephant and the bush cow, and throwing his bow and arrows away, ran and hid himself in the bush. About six hours later, both the elephant and bush cow died in great pain.

Ever since, when wild animals want to fight between themselves, they always fight in the big bush and not on the public roads. And as the fight was never definitely decided between the elephant and the bush cow, they fight whenever they meet each other in the forest, even to the present time.

Comment [kC]: Why did the chief need to hide after killing the animals?

THE ROOSTER WHO CAUSED A FIGHT BETWEEN TWO TOWNS

Ekpo and Etim were half-brothers, that is to say they had the same mother but different fathers. Their mother had first married a chief of Duke Town, where Ekpo was born; but after a time she got tired of him and went to Old Town, where she married Ejuqua and gave birth to Etim.

Both of the boys grew up and became very rich. Ekpo had a rooster of which he was very fond, and every day when he sat down to eat the rooster would fly on the table to feed also. Ama Ukwa was a poor man and a native of Old Town. Though he pretended to be friends with the two brothers, he was very jealous of them and made up his mind to bring about a quarrel between them.

One day, Ekpo, the older brother, gave a big feast to which Etim and many other people were invited. Ama Ukwa was also present. A very good dinner was laid for the guests and a great deal of palm wine was provided. When they started to eat, the pet rooster flew on to the table and began to feed off Etim's plate. Etim then told one of his servants to seize the rooster and tie him up in the house until after the feast. So the servant carried the rooster to Etim's house and tied him up for safety.

After much eating and drinking, Etim returned home late at night with his friend, Ama Ukwa, and just before they went to bed, Ama Ukwa saw Ekpo's rooster tied up. Early in the morning, Ama Ukwa went to Ekpo's house and he was gladly received. About eight o'clock, when it was time for Ekpo to have his early morning meal, he noticed that his pet rooster was missing. When he remarked upon its absence, Ama Ukwa told him that his brother had seized the rooster the previous evening during dinner and was going to kill it just to see what Ekpo would do. Ekpo was very vexed when he heard this and he sent Ama Ukwa back to his brother to ask him to return the rooster immediately. Instead of delivering the message as he had been instructed, Ama Ukwa told Etim that his elder brother was so angry with him for taking away the rooster, that he would fight him and had sent Ama Ukwa on purpose to declare war between the two towns.

Etim then told Ama Ukwa to return to Ekpo and say he would be prepared for anything his brother could do. Ama Ukwa advised Ekpo to call all his people in from their farms as Etim would attack him, and on his return he advised Etim to do the same. He then arranged a day for the fight to take place between the two brothers and their people. On the day of the fight, Etim marched his men to the other side of the creek and waited for his brother. Ekpo then led his men against his brother and there was a big battle, with many men killed on both sides. The fighting went on all day until at last towards evening, the other chiefs of Calabar met and determined to stop it. They called the *Ekpe* men together and sent them out with their drums, and eventually the fight stopped.

Three days later, a big meeting was held where each of the brothers was told to state his case. When they had done so, it was found that Ama Ukwa had caused the quarrel so the chiefs ordered that he should be killed. His father, who was a rich man, offered to give the *Ekpes* five thousand rods, five cows, and seven slaves to redeem his son but they refused his offer. The next day, after being severely flogged, he was left for twenty-four hours tied up to a tree before his head was cut off.

Ekpo was then ordered to kill his pet rooster so that it should not cause any further trouble between himself and his brother; and a law was passed that for the future no one should keep a pet rooster or any other domestic animal.

WHY THE HIPPOPOTAMUS LIVES IN THE WATER

Comment [kC]: Choose one, the latter preferably

Many years ago, the hippopotamus, whose name was Isantim, was one of the biggest kings on the land; he was second only to the elephant. The hippo had seven large fat wives of whom he was very fond. Now and then he used to give a big feast to the people but a curious thing was that although everyone knew the hippo, no one, except his seven wives, knew his name.

At one of the feasts, just as the people were about to sit down, the hippo said, "You have come to feed at my table but none of you know my name. If you cannot tell my name, you shall all go away without your dinner."

As they could not guess his name, they had to go away and leave all the good food and *tombo* behind. But before they left, the tortoise stood up and asked the hippopotamus what he would do if he told him his name at the next feast. The hippo replied that he would be so ashamed of himself that he and his whole family would leave the land, and for the future would dwell in the river.

Now it was custom for the hippo and his seven wives to go down every morning and evening to the river to wash and have a drink. Of this custom the tortoise was aware. The hippo used to walk first and the seven wives followed. One day, when they had gone down to the river to bathe, the tortoise made a small hole in the middle of the path and then waited. On their return, two of the hippo's wives were some distance behind. The tortoise came out from where he had been hiding and half buried himself in the hole he had dug, leaving the greater part of his shell exposed. As the two hippo wives came along, the first one knocked her foot against the tortoise's shell and immediately called out to her husband, "Oh! Isantim, my husband, I have hurt my foot." At this the tortoise was very glad, and went joyfully home, as he had found out the hippo's name.

When the next feast was given by the hippo, he made the same condition about his name. And the tortoise got up and said, "Do you promise you will not kill me if I tell you your name?" The hippo promised. The tortoise then shouted as loud as he was able, "Your name is Isantim!" at which a cheer went up from all the people, and then they sat down to their dinner.

After the feast, the hippo with his seven wives, to fulfill his promise, went down to the river where they have always lived from that day till now. And although they come on shore to feed at night, you can never find a hippo on the land in the daytime.

THE STORY OF
THE FAT WOMAN
WHO MELTED AWAY

There was once a very fat woman who was made of oil. She was very beautiful and many young men approached her parents for permission to marry their daughter and offered dowry but the mother always refused. She said it was impossible for her daughter to work on a farm, as she would melt in the sun. At last, a stranger came from a far distant country and fell in love with the fat woman and promised her mother he would always keep her in the shade if he allowed him to marry her daughter. At last the mother agreed, and he took his wife away.

When he arrived at his house, his other wife immediately became very jealous because when there was work to be done, firewood to be collected, or water to be carried, the fat woman stayed at home and never helped as she was afraid of the heat. One day, when the husband was absent, the jealous wife abused the fat woman so much that she finally agreed to go and work on the farm. Her little sister, whom she had brought from home with her, implored her not to go, reminding her that their mother had always told them ever

64

since they were born that she would melt away if she went into the sun.

All the way to the farm, the fat woman managed to keep in the shade and when they arrived at the farm the sun was very hot, so the fat woman remained in the shade of a big tree. When the jealous wife saw this, she again began to abuse her and asked her why she did not do her share of the work. At last she could stand the nagging no longer, and although her little sister tried very hard to prevent her, the fat woman went out into the sun to work and immediately began to melt away. There was very soon nothing left of her but one big toe which had been covered by a leaf. Her little sister saw this and with tears in her eyes, she picked up the toe, which was all that remained of the fat woman, covered it carefully with leaves and placed it in the bottom of her basket. When she arrived at the house, the little sister placed the toe in a clay pot, filled it with water and covered the top up with clay.

When the husband returned, he said, "Where is my fat wife?" and the little sister, crying bitterly, told him that the jealous woman had made her go out into the sun and that she had melted away. She then showed him the pot with the remains of her sister, and told him that her sister would come to life again in three months' time quite complete, but he must send away the jealous wife so that there would be no more trouble. If he refused to do this, the little girl said, she would take the pot back to their mother and when her sister became complete again they would remain at home.

The husband then took the jealous wife back to her parents who sold her as a slave and paid the dowry back to the man so that he could get another wife. As soon as he received the money, the husband took it home and kept it until the three months had elapsed. When the little sister opened the pot, the fat woman emerged, quite as fat and beautiful as she had been before. The husband was so delighted that he gave a feast to all his friends and neighbors and told them the whole story of the bad behavior of his jealous wife.

Ever since that time, whenever a wife behaves very badly, the husband returns her to her parents who would sell the woman as a slave and out of the proceeds of the sale, reimburse the husband the amount of dowry he paid when he married the girl.

THE LEOPARD, THE SQUIRREL, AND THE TORTOISE

Many years ago, there was a great famine throughout the land and all the people were starving. The yam crop had failed entirely, the plantains did not bear any fruit, the groundnuts were all shriveled up, and the corn never grew; even the palm-oil nuts did not ripen, and the peppers and okras also dried up.

However, the leopard, who lived entirely on beef, did not care for any of these things. And although some of the animals who lived on corn and other cultivated crops began to get rather skinny, he did not mind very much. In order to save himself trouble, as everybody was complaining of the famine, he called a meeting of all the animals and told them that as they all knew, he was very powerful and must have food, that the famine did not affect him as he only lived on flesh and as there were a lot of animals about, he did not intend to starve.

He told all the animals present at the meeting that if they did not wish to be killed themselves they must bring their grandmothers to him for food, and when they were finished he would feed off their mothers. He told them that they may bring their grandmothers one after the other and he would take them in their turn; so that as there were many different animals, it would probably be some time before their mothers were eaten, by which time it was possible that the famine would be over. He warned them that he was determined to have sufficient food for himself, and that if the grandmothers or mothers were not forthcoming he would turn upon the young people themselves and kill and eat them. The young generation who had attended the meeting did not appreciate this and in order to save their own skins, agreed to supply the leopard with his daily meal.

The first to appear with his aged grandmother was the squirrel. The grandmother was a poor decrepit old thing with a little tail, and the leopard swallowed her at one gulp and then looked round for more. In an angry voice he growled out, "This is not the proper food for me; I must have more at once. Then a bush cat pushed his old grandmother in front of the leopard but he snarled at her and said, "Take the nasty old thing away; I want some sweet food."

It was then the turn of a bush buck, and after so much hesitation, a wretchedly poor and thin old doe tottered and fell in front of the leopard who immediately killed her. And although the meal was very unsatisfactory, he declared that his appetite was satisfied for that day.

The Foo-Foo Tree and more Efik Folktales

The next day, a few more animals brought their old grandmothers until at last it became the tortoise's turn. But being very cunning, he produced witnesses to prove that his grandmother was dead, so the leopard excused him.

After a few days, all the animals' grandmothers were finished, and it became the turn of the mothers to supply food for the ravenous leopard. Now although most of the young animals did not mind getting rid of their grandmothers whom they had scarcely even known, many of them had very strong objections to providing, as food for the leopard, their mothers of whom they were very fond.

The strongest objections came from the squirrel and the tortoise. The tortoise, who had thought the whole thing out, was aware that as everyone knew that his mother was alive (she being rather an amiable old person and friendly with all-comers), the same excuse would not avail him a second time. He therefore told his mother to climb up a palm tree and that he would provide her with food until the famine was over. He instructed her to let down a basket every day and said that he would place food in it for her. The tortoise made the basket for his mother and attached it to a long string of *tie-tie*. The string was so strong that she could haul her son up whenever he wished to visit her.

Comment [kC]: What about the tortoise's grandmother? If he is hiding his mother, where is his grandmother?

69

All went well for some days as the tortoise used to go at daylight to the bottom of the tree where his mother lived and place her food in the basket. Then the old lady would pull the basket up and have her food and the tortoise would depart on his daily round in his usual leisurely manner.

In the meantime, the leopard had to have his regular food and the squirrel's turn came first after the grandmothers had been finished. As he was a poor, weak thing and not very wise, he was forced to produce his mother for the leopard to eat. The squirrel was, however, very fond of his mother, and when she had been eaten he remembered that the tortoise had not produced his grandmother for the leopard's food. He therefore determined to set a watch on the movements of the tortoise.

The very next morning, while he was gathering nuts, he saw the tortoise walking very slowly through the bush, and being high up in the trees and able to travel very fast, had no difficulty in keeping the tortoise in sight without being noticed. When the tortoise arrived at the foot of the tree where his mother lived, he placed the food in the basket which his mother had let down already by the *tie-tie*. Having got into the basket and given a pull at the string to signify that everything was right, he was hauled up and after a time was let down again in the basket. The squirrel was watching all the time, and as soon as the tortoise had gone, jumped from branch to branch of the trees and very soon arrived at the place where the leopard was snoozing.

When he woke up, the squirrel said, "You have eaten my grandmother and my mother, but the tortoise has not provided any food for you. It is now his turn and he has hidden his mother away in a tree." At this the leopard was very angry, and told the squirrel to lead him at once to the tree where the tortoise's mother lived. But the squirrel said, "The tortoise only goes at daylight when his mother lets down a basket; so if you go early in the morning, she will pull you up and you can then kill her." To this the leopard agreed, and the next morning, the squirrel came at roostercrow and led the leopard to the tree where the tortoise's mother was hidden.

The old lady had already let down the basket for her daily supply of food, and the leopard got into it and gave the line a pull. But except for a few small jerks, nothing happened as the old mother tortoise was not strong enough to pull a heavy leopard off the ground. When the leopard saw that he was not going to be pulled up, being an expert climber, he scrambled up the tree. He found the poor old tortoise on top of the tree with a shell so tough that he thought she was not worth eating. He threw her down to the ground in a violent temper and then came down himself and went home.

Shortly after this, the tortoise arrived at the tree and finding the basket on the ground, gave his usual tug at it but there was no answer. He then looked about and after a little time, came upon the broken shell of his poor old mother who by this time was quite dead. The tortoise knew at once that the leopard had killed his mother and made up his mind that for the future he would live alone and have nothing to do with the other animals.

THE LEOPARD, THE TORTOISE, AND THE BUSH RAT

At the time of the great famine, all the animals were very thin and weak from want of food. But there was one exception - the tortoise and his family members who were quite fat and did not seem to suffer at all. Even the leopard was very thin in spite of the arrangement he had made with the animals to bring him their old grandmothers and mothers for food.

In the early days of the famine (as you will remember), the leopard had killed the tortoise's mother, and because of this the tortoise was very angry with the leopard and determined to revenge upon him. The tortoise, who was very clever, had discovered a shallow lake full of fish in the middle of the forest. Every morning, he would go to the lake and without much trouble, bring back enough food for himself and his family.

One day, the leopard met the tortoise and noticed how fat he was. As he was very thin himself, he decided to watch the tortoise. So the next morning, he hid himself in the long grass near the tortoise's house and waited very patiently until at last the tortoise came along quite slowly, carrying a basket which appeared to be very heavy. Then

74

the leopard leapt out and said to the tortoise, "What have you got in that basket?" The tortoise, as he did not want to lose his breakfast, replied that he was carrying firewood back to his home. Unfortunately for the tortoise, the leopard had a very acute sense of smell and knew at once that there was fish in the basket, so he said, "I know there is fish in there, and I am going to eat it."

The tortoise, not being in a position to refuse as he was such a poor creature, said, "Very well. Let us sit down under this shady tree, and if you will make a fire I will go to my house and get pepper, oil, and salt, and then we will feed together."

To this the leopard agreed and began to search about for dry wood to start the fire. Meanwhile, the tortoise waddled off to his house and very soon returned with the pepper, salt, and oil. He also brought a long piece of very strong cane *tie-tie*. This he put on the ground and began boiling the fish. Then he said to the leopard, "While we are waiting for the fish to cook, let us play at tying one another up to a tree. You may tie me up first and when I say "Tighten", you must lose the rope, and when I say "Loosen", you must tighten the rope."

The leopard, who was very hungry, thought that this game would make the time pass more quickly until the fish was cooked, so

75

he said he would play. The tortoise then stood with his back to the tree and said, "Loosen the rope" and the leopard, in accordance with the rules of the game, began to tie up the tortoise. Very soon the tortoise shouted out, "Tighten!" and the leopard at once unfastened the *tie-tie*, and the tortoise was free. The tortoise then said, "Now, leopard, it is your turn."

The leopard stood up against the tree and called out to the tortoise to loosen the rope, and the tortoise at once very quickly passed the rope several times round the leopard and got him fast to the tree. Then the leopard said, "Tighten the rope", but instead of playing the game in accordance with the rules he had laid down, the tortoise ran faster and faster with the rope round the leopard, taking great care however, to keep out of reach of the leopard's claws. And very soon he had the leopard so securely fastened that it was quite impossible for him to free himself.

All this time, the leopard was calling out to the tortoise to let him go as he was tired of the game but the tortoise only laughed and sat down at the fireside and commenced his meal. When he had finished, he packed up the remainder of the fish for his family and prepared to go. But before he left he said to the leopard, "You killed my mother and now you want to take my fish. It is not likely that I am going to the lake to get fish for you, so I shall leave you here to starve."

He then threw the remains of the pepper and salt into the leopard's eyes and quietly went on his way, leaving the leopard roaring with pain. All that day and throughout the night, the leopard called out for someone to release him and vowed all sorts of vengeance on the tortoise, but no one came as the people and animals of the forest did not like to hear the leopard's voice.

In the morning, when the animals began to go about to get their food, the leopard called out to everyone he saw to come and untie him, but they all refused as they knew that if they did so the leopard would most likely kill and eat them. At last, a bush rat came near and saw the leopard tied up to the tree and asked him what the matter was. The leopard explained to him that he had been playing a game of "tight and loose" with the tortoise and that the tortoise had tied him up and left him there to starve. The leopard then implored the bush rat to cut the ropes with his sharp teeth.

The bush rat was very sorry for the leopard but at the same time he knew that if he let the leopard go, he would most likely be killed and eaten so he hesitated and said that he did not quite see his way to cutting the ropes. But this bush rat, being rather kind-hearted and having had some experience of traps himself, could empathize with the leopard in his uncomfortable position. He therefore thought for a time and then hit upon a plan. He first started to dig a hole under the tree, quite regardless of the leopard's cries. When he had finished digging, he came out, cut one of the ropes and immediately ran into his hole and waited there to see what would happen. But although the leopard struggled frantically, he could not get loose as the tortoise had tied him up very tightly. After a time, when he saw that there was no danger, the bush rat crept out again and very carefully bit through another rope, and then retired to his hole as before. Again nothing happened, and he began to feel more confidence, so he bit several strands through, one after the other, until at last the leopard was free.

The leopard, who was ravenous with hunger, instead of being grateful to the bush rat, made a dash at him with his big paw immediately he was free but missed as the bush rat had dived for his hole. However, he was not quite quick enough to escape and the leopard's sharp claws slashed his back and left marks which he carried to his grave. Ever since then, bush rats have had white spots on their skins, which represent the marks of the leopard's claws.

THE KING
AND THE JUJU TREE

Udo Ubok Udom was a famous king who lived at Itam, which is an inland town, and does not possess a river. The king and his wife therefore used to wash at the spring just behind their house. King Udo had a daughter of whom he was very fond and looked after most carefully, and she grew up into a beautiful woman.

For some time, the king had been absent from his house and had not been to the spring for two years. When he went to his old place to wash, he found that the Idem *Juju* tree had grown up all round the place and it was impossible for him to use the spring as he had done before. He therefore called fifty of his young men to bring their machetes to cut down the tree. But it was a fruitless effort as immediately they made a cut in the tree, it closed up again. After working all day, they could not cut down the tree.

They returned at night and told the king that they had been unable to destroy the tree. He was very angry when he heard this and went to the spring the following morning, taking his own machete with him. When the *Juju* tree saw that the king had come himself and was trying to cut his branches, he caused a small splinter of wood to

79

go into the king's eye. This gave the king great pain, so he threw down his machete and went back to his house. The pain, however, got worse and he could not eat or sleep for three days. He therefore sent for his witch men and told them to cast lots to find out why he was in such pain.

When they had cast lots, they decided that the reason was that the *Juju* tree was angry with the king because he wanted to wash at the spring and had tried to destroy the tree.

They then told the king that he must take seven baskets of flies, a white goat, a white chicken, and a piece of white cloth, and make a sacrifice with them in order to pacify the *Juju*. The king did this and the witch men tried their lotions on the king's eye but it got worse. He then dismissed these witches and got another set who told the king that although they could do nothing themselves to relieve his pain, they knew one man who lived in the spirit land who could cure him. So the king told them to send for him at once, and he arrived the next day.

Then the spirit man said, "Before I do anything to your eye, what will you give me?" So King Udo said, "I will give you half my town with the people in it, also seven cows and some money." But the spirit man refused to accept the king's offer. As the king was in such pain, he said, "Name your own price, and I will pay you." So the spirit man said the only thing he was willing to accept as payment was the king's daughter. At this the king cried very much and told the man to go away, as he would rather die than let him have his daughter.

That night, the pain was worse than ever and some of his subjects pleaded with the king to send for the spirit man again and give him his daughter; and told him that when he got well he could have another daughter but that if he died now he would lose everything. The king then sent for the spirit man again, who came very quickly, and in great grief the king handed his daughter to the spirit.

The spirit man then went out into the bush and collected some leaves which he soaked in water and beat up. He poured the juice into the king's eye and told him that when he washed his face in the morning he would be able to see what was troubling him in the eye. The king tried to persuade him to stay the night, but the spirit man refused and departed that same night for the spirit land, taking the king's daughter with him.

Before it was light, the king rose up and washed his face and the small splinter from the *Juju* tree which had been troubling him so much, dropped out of his eye. The pain disappeared and he was quite well again. When he came to his senses, he realized that he had sacrificed his daughter for one of his eyes, so he made an order that there should be general mourning throughout his kingdom for three years.

For the first two years of the mourning, the king's daughter was put in the fattening house by the spirit man and was given food. But a skull who was in the house told her not to eat as they were fattening her up, not for marriage, but so that they could eat her. She therefore gave all the food which was brought to her to the skull and lived on chalk herself. Towards the end of the third year, the spirit man brought some of his friends to see the king's daughter, and told them he would kill her the next day, and they would have a good feast of her.

When she woke up in the morning, the spirit man brought her food as usual but the skull, who wanted to preserve her life and who had heard what the spirit man had said, called her into the room and told her what was going to happen later in the day. She handed the food to the skull and he said, "When the spirit man goes to the wood with his friends to prepare for the feast, you must run back to your father."

He then gave her some medicine which would make her strong for the journey, and also gave her directions as to the road. He told her that there were two roads and when she came to the parting of the roads, she should drop some of the medicine on the ground and the two roads would become one. He told her to leave by the back door and go through the wood until she came to the end of the town where she would find the roads. She was told to pass everyone she met on the road in silence, as if she greeted them they would know that she was a stranger in the spirit land and might kill her. She was also not to turn round if anyone called her, but was to go straight on till she reached her father's house.

Having thanked the skull for his kind advice, the king's daughter started off and when she reached the end of the town and found the road, she ran for three hours and at last arrived at the branch roads. There she dropped the medicine as she had been instructed and the two roads immediately became one; so she went straight on and never greeted anyone or turned back, although several people called out to her.

About this time, the spirit man had returned from the wood and went to the house only to find the king's daughter was absent. He asked the skull where she was and he replied that she had gone out by the back door but he did not know where she had gone to. Being a spirit, however, he sensed that she had gone home so he followed as quickly as possible, shouting out all the time.

The girl heard his voice and ran as fast as she could till she arrived at her father's house. She told him to quickly take a cow, a pig, a sheep, a goat, a dog, a chicken and seven eggs, and cut them into seven parts as a sacrifice, and leave them on the road so that when the spirit man saw these things he would stop and not enter the town. The king immediately made the sacrifice as his daughter had told him.

When the spirit man saw the sacrifice on the road, he sat down and at once began to eat. After he had satisfied his appetite, he packed up the leftovers and returned to the spirit land, not worrying anymore about the king's daughter. When the king saw that the danger was over, he beat his drum and declared that for the future, when people died and went to the spirit land, they should not come to earth again as spirits to cure sick people.

THE TORTOISE, THE ELEPHANT AND THE HIPPOPOTAMUS

The elephant and the hippopotamus always used to feed together and were good friends. One day when they were both dining together, the tortoise appeared and said that although they were both big and strong, neither of them could pull him out of the water with a strong piece of *tie-tie*, and he offered the elephant ten thousand rods if he could draw him out of the river the next day. The elephant, seeing that the tortoise was very small, said, "If I cannot draw you out of the water, I will give you twenty thousand rods."

The following morning, the tortoise got some very strong *tie-tie*, fastened it to his leg and went down to the river. When he got there, as he knew the place well, he looped the *tie-tie* round a big rock, and left the other end on the shore for the elephant to pull by, then went down to the bottom of the river and hid himself. The elephant came down and started pulling and after a time he broke the rope.

Immediately this happened, the tortoise undid the rope from the rock and came to land, showing all people that the rope was still fastened to his leg but that the elephant had failed to pull him out. The elephant was thus forced to admit that the tortoise was the winner, and paid him the twenty thousand rods as agreed. The tortoise then took the rods home to his wife and they were very happy.

After three months, the tortoise, seeing that the money was greatly reduced, thought he would make some more by the same trick, so he went to the hippopotamus and made the same bet with him. The hippopotamus said, "I will make the bet but I shall take the water and you shall take the land, I will then pull you into the water." To this the tortoise agreed, so they went down to the river as before, and having got some strong *tie-tie*, the tortoise tied it to the hippopotamus' hind leg and told him to go into the water. Immediately the hippo turned his back and left, the tortoise took the rope twice round a strong palm-tree which was growing nearby, and then hid himself at the foot of the tree.

When the hippo was tired of pulling, he came up puffing and blowing water into the air from his nostrils. Immediately the tortoise saw him coming up, he unwound the rope and walked down towards the hippopotamus, showing him the *tie-tie* round his leg. The hippo had to acknowledge that the tortoise was too strong for him and handed over the twenty thousand rods.

The elephant and the hippo were quite amazed at the strength of the tortoise despite his small size, and from that day they had more regard for him.

Comment [kC]: Why did you delete the part of this story? I think what we have now ended too abruptly. I think we should add if it is only that the tortoise became friends with the elephant and the hippopotamus and they lived happily ever after. Or consider t added line.

THE PRETTY GIRL AND THE SEVEN JEALOUS WOMEN

There was once a very beautiful girl called Akim. She was a native of Ibibio. Her name was given to her on account of her good looks, as she was born in the spring time. She was an only daughter and her parents were extremely fond of her. The people of the town, and more particularly the young girls, were very jealous of Akim's good looks and beautiful form - for she was perfectly made, very strong, and her posture, walking and manners were very graceful. Her parents would not allow her to join the young girls' society in the town as is customary for all young people to do. As a rule, both boys and girls belonged to a company consisting of all those born in the same year, according to their age.

Akim's parents were poor but she was a good daughter and gave them no trouble, so they had a happy home. One day, as Akim was on her way to draw water from the spring, she met seven girls who were members of a group she would have belonged to if her parents had not forbidden her. These girls told her that they were going to hold a play in the town in three days' time and asked her to join them. She said she was very sorry, but that her parents were poor and she was the only one who worked for them and so she had no time to spare for dancing and playing. She then left them and went home.

In the evening, the seven girls met together, and as they were very envious of Akim, they discussed how they could revenge on her for refusing to join their group. They talked for a long time as to how they could get Akim into danger or punish her in some way. At last, one of the girls suggested that they should all go to Akim's house every day and help her with her chores, so that when they had made friends with her they would be able to entice her away and take their revenge upon her for being more beautiful than themselves. Although they went every day and helped Akim and her parents with their work, the parents knew that the girls were jealous of their daughter and repeatedly warned her not to, on any account, go with them anywhere as they were not to be trusted.

At the end of the year, there was going to be a big festival called the New Yam festival to which Akim's parents were invited. The festival was going to be held at a town about two hours' walk from where they lived. Akim was very anxious to go and take part in the festival but her parents gave her a lot of work to do before they started, thinking that this would surely prevent her from going to the festival. They knew she was a very obedient girl and she always did her work properly.

On the morning of the festival, the seven jealous girls came to Akim and asked her to go with them. She pointed to all the water pots she had to fill and showed them where her parents had told her to polish the walls with a stone and make the floor good; and after that was finished she had to pull up all the weeds round the house and clean up all round. She therefore said it was impossible for her to leave the house until all the work was finished. When the girls heard this, they took up the water pots, went to the spring and quickly returned with them full. And then they got stones and very soon had the walls polished and the floor made good; after that they did the weeding outside and the cleaning up. When everything was completed, they said to Akim, "Now then, come along. You have no excuse to remain behind as all the work is done." Akim really wanted to go to the festival and as all the chores her parents gave her to do were done, she finally consented to go.

About half-way to the town where the New Yam festival was being held, there was a small river about five feet deep which had to be crossed by wading through it as there was no bridge. In this river was a powerful *Juju* whose law was that whenever anyone crossed the river, whoever it was had to give some food to the *Juju* on the return journey. If they did not make the proper sacrifice, the *Juju* dragged them down and took them to his home and kept them there to work for him. The seven jealous girls knew all about this *Juju*, having often crossed the river before, as they walked about all over the country and had a lot of friends in different towns. Akim, however, who was a good girl and never went anywhere, knew nothing about this *Juju*.

When the work was finished, they all started off together and crossed the river without any trouble. After they had gone a small distance on the other side, they saw a small bird perched on a high tree. The bird admired Akim very much and sang in praise of her beauty, much to the annoyance of the seven girls. But they walked on without saying anything and eventually arrived at the town where the play was being held.

Akim had not taken the trouble to change her clothes, but when she arrived at the town, although her companions had on all their best beads and their finest clothes, the young men and people admired Akim far more than the other girls and she was declared to be the finest and most beautiful woman at the dance. They gave her lots of palm wine, *foo-foo* and everything she wanted, and this made the seven girls more angry and jealous. The people danced and sang all night and Akim managed to keep out of the sight of her parents until the following morning. They asked her how it was that she had disobeyed them and neglected her work. Akim told them that the work had all been done by her friends and they had persuaded her to come to the festival with them. Her mother then told her to return home at once, and that she was not to remain in the town any longer.

When Akim told her friends, they said, "Very well, we are just going to have some small meal and then we will return with you." They all then sat down together and had their food, but each of the seven jealous girls hid a small quantity of *foo-foo* and fish in her clothes for the Water *Juju*. However, Akim, who knew nothing about this, did not take any food as a sacrifice to the *Juju* with her. And her parents forgot to tell her about the *Juju*, since they never thought that their daughter would cross the river.

At the river, Akim saw the girls making their small sacrifices and begged them to give her a small share so that she could do the same, but they refused and all of them walked across the river safely. Then when it was Akim's turn to cross, the Water *Juju* caught hold of her when she arrived in the middle of the river and dragged her underneath the water, so that she immediately disappeared from sight.

The seven girls had been watching for this and when they saw that she had gone they went on their way, very pleased at the success of their scheme and said to one another, "Now Akim is gone forever, and we shall hear no more about her being better-looking than we are."

As there was no one to be seen at the time when Akim disappeared, they naturally thought that their cruel action had escaped detection so they went home rejoicing. But they never noticed the little bird high up in the tree who had sung of Akim's beauty when they were on their way to the festival. The little bird was very sorry for Akim and made up his mind that when the proper time came, he would tell her parents what he had seen, so that perhaps they would be able to save her. The bird had heard Akim asking for a small portion of the food to make a sacrifice with and had heard all the girls refusing to give her any.

The following morning, when Akim's parents returned home, they were much surprised to find that the door was locked and that there was no sign of their daughter anywhere about the place. They inquired of their neighbors but no one was able to give them any information about her. They then went to the seven girls and asked them what had become of Akim. The girls said they did not know what had become of her, but that she had reached their town safely with them and then said she was going home.

Akim's father then went to his *Juju* man, who, by casting lots, discovered what had happened and told him that on her way back from the play Akim had crossed the river without making the customary sacrifice to the Water *Juju*, and that as the *Juju* was angry, he had seized Akim and taken her to his home. He therefore told Akim's father to take one goat, one basketful of eggs, and one piece of white cloth to the river in the morning, and to offer them as a sacrifice to the Water *Juju*; then Akim would be thrown out of the water seven times, but that if her father failed to catch her on the seventh time, she would disappear forever.

When Akim's father returned home, the little bird who had seen Akim taken by the Water *Juju*, told him everything that happened, confirming the *Juju*'s words. He also said that it was entirely the fault of the seven girls, who had refused to give Akim any food to make the sacrifice with.

Early the following morning, Akim's parents went to the river and made the sacrifice as advised by the *Juju*. Immediately they had done so, the Water *Juju* threw Akim up from the middle of the river. Her father caught her at once and returned home thankfully. He didn't tell anyone that he had got his daughter back but made up his mind to punish the seven jealous girls. He dug a deep pit in the middle of his house and placed dried palm leaves and sharp stakes in the bottom of the pit. He then covered the top of the pit with new mats and sent out word for people to come and hold a play to rejoice with him as his daughter had returned from the spirit land. Many people came, danced and sang all day and night, but the seven jealous girls did not appear as they were frightened.

However, as they were told that everything had gone well the previous day and that there was no trouble, they went to the house the following morning and mixed with the dancers. Akim was sitting down in the middle of the dancing ring but they were ashamed to look her in the face. When Akim's father saw the seven girls, he pretended to welcome them as his daughter's friends, and presented each of them with a brass rod which he placed round their necks. He also gave them *tombo* to drink. He then picked them out and told them to go and sit on mats on the other side of the pit he had prepared for them. As they walked over the mats which hid the pit, they all fell in and Akim's father immediately got some red-hot ashes from the fire and threw them in on top of the screaming girls. At once, the dried palm leaves caught fire, killing all the girls. When the people heard the cries and saw the smoke, they all ran back to the town.

The next day, the parents of the dead girls went to the head chief and complained that Akim's father had killed their daughters, so the chief called him and asked him for an explanation. Akim's father went to the chief, taking the *Juju* man whom everybody relied on, and the small bird, as his witnesses. After the chief had heard the whole case, he told Akim's father that he should only have killed one girl to avenge his daughter and not seven. So he told the father to bring Akim before him. When she arrived, the head chief, seeing how beautiful she was, said that her father was justified in killing all the seven girls. He dismissed the case and told the parents of the dead girls to go away and mourn their daughters who were wicked and jealous women and had been properly punished for their cruel behavior to Akim.

THE ORPHAN BOY
AND THE MAGIC STONE

A chief of Inde named Inkita had a son named Ayong Kita whose mother had died at his birth. The old chief was a hunter and used to take his son out with him when he went into the bush. He did most of his hunting in the long grass which grows over nearly all the Inde country and killed so many bush bucks in the dry season.

In those days, the people had no guns so the chief had to shoot everything he got with his bow and arrows, which required a lot of skill. When his little son was old enough, he gave him a small bow and some small arrows and taught him how to shoot. The little boy was very quick at learning and by continually practicing at shooting lizards and small birds, he soon became an expert in the use of his little bow and could hit them almost every time he shot at them.

When the boy was ten years old, his father died and he thus became the head of his father's house and was in authority over all the slaves. They became very discontented and made plans to kill him so he ran away into the bush. Having nothing to eat, he lived for several days on the nuts which fell from palm trees. He was too young to kill any large animals and only had his small bow and arrows with which he killed a few squirrels, bush rats and small birds, and so managed to live.

One night when he was sleeping in the hollow of a tree, he had a dream in which his father appeared and told him where there was a great deal of treasure buried in the earth; but being a small boy, he was frightened and did not go to the place. One day, sometime after the dream, having walked far and being very thirsty, he went to a lake and was just going to drink when he heard a hissing sound and a voice telling him not to drink. Not seeing anyone, he was afraid and ran away without drinking.

Early the next morning, when he was out with his bow trying to shoot some small animals, he met an old woman with a very long hair. She was so ugly that he thought he must be a witch. He tried to run but she told him not to fear, as she wanted to help him and assist him to rule over his late father's house. She also told him that it was she who had called out to him at the lake not to drink, that there was a bad *Juju* in the water which would have killed him. The old woman then took Ayong to a stream some little distance from the lake, and bending down, took out a small shining stone from the water. She gave the stone to him and told him to go to the place which his father had advised him to visit in his dream.

She then said, "When you get there you must dig, and you will find a lot of money. You must then go and buy two strong slaves and when you have got them, you must take them into the forest, away from the town, and get them to build you a house with several rooms in it. You must then place the stone in one of the rooms and whenever you want anything, all you have to do is to go into the room and tell the stone what you want and your wishes will be at once granted."

Ayong did as the old woman told him, and after much difficulty and danger, bought the two slaves and built a house in the forest, taking great care of the precious stone which he placed in an inner room. Then for some time, whenever he wanted anything, he would go into the room and ask for a sufficient number of rods to buy what he wanted, and they were always brought at once.

This went on for many years and Ayong grew up to be a man and became very rich. He bought many slaves, having made friends with the Aro men who, in those days, used to do a big trade in slaves. After ten years, Ayong had a large town and many slaves. One night, the old woman appeared to him in a dream and told him that he was sufficiently wealthy, and that it was time for him to return the magic stone to the small stream from where it came.

But Ayong, although he was rich, wanted to rule his father's house and be a head chief for all the Inde country, so he sent for all the *Juju* men in the country and two witch men and marched with all his slaves to his father's town. Before he started, he held a big meeting and told them to point out any slave who had a bad heart and who might kill him when he came to rule the country. The *Juju* men consulted together and pointed out fifty of the slaves who they said were witches and would try to kill Ayong. He at once had them made prisoners and tried them by the ordeal of the Esere bean to see whether they were witches or not. As none of them could vomit the beans, they all died and were declared to be witches. He then had them buried at once.

When the rest of his slaves saw what had happened, they all came to him and begged his pardon and promised to serve him faithfully. Although the fifty men were buried, they could not rest and they troubled Ayong very much. After a time, Ayong became very sick and sent again for the *Juju* men who told him that it was the witch men who, although they were dead and buried, had power to come out at night and used to suck Ayong's blood and this was the cause of his sickness.

They then said, "We are only three *Juju* men; you must get seven more of us, making the magic number of ten." When they came, they dug up the bodies of the fifty witches and found they were quite fresh. Then Ayong had big fires made and burned them one after the other, and gave the *Juju* men a big present. He soon became quite well again, took possession of his father's property, and ruled over all the country.

Ever since then, whenever anyone is accused of being a witch, they are tried by the ordeal of the poisonous Esere bean, and if they can vomit they do not die, and are declared innocent, but if they cannot do so, they die in great pain.

THE SLAVE GIRL WHO TRIED
TO KILL HER MISTRESS

A man called Akpan, who was a native of Oku, a town in the Ibibio country, admired a girl called Emme very much and wished to marry her. Emme lived at Ibibio and was the finest girl among her peers. It was the custom in those days for parents to demand a large amount as dowries for their daughters and if after they were married they failed to get on with their husbands, they were sold as slaves as they could not redeem themselves. Akpan paid a very large sum as dowry for Emme and she was put in the fattening house until the proper time arrived for her to marry.

Akpan told Emme's parents that when their daughter was ready they must send her over to him and they promised to do so. Emme's father was a rich man and after seven years had elapsed and it was time for Emme to go to her husband, he saw a very fine girl who had also just come out of the fattening house and whom the parents wished to sell as a slave. Emme's father therefore bought her and gave her to his daughter as her handmaiden.

The next day, Emme's little sister, being very anxious to go with her, obtained the consent of her mother and they started off together, the slave girl carrying a large bundle containing clothes and presents from Emme's father. Akpan's house was a long day's march from where they lived. When they arrived just outside the town, they came to a spring where the people used to get their drinking water from but no one was allowed to bathe there. Emme, however, knew nothing about this. They took off their clothes to wash close to the spring and where there was a deep hole which led to the Water *Juju*'s house.

The slave girl knew of this *Juju* and thought if she could get her mistress to bathe, she would be taken by the *Juju* and she would then be able to take her place and marry Akpan. So they went down to bathe and when they were close to the water, the slave girl pushed her mistress in and she at once disappeared. The little girl then began to cry but the slave girl said, "If you cry any more I will kill you and throw your body into the hole after your sister." And she told the child that she must never mention what had happened to anyone, and particularly not to Akpan as she was going to represent her sister and marry him; and that if she ever told anyone what she had seen, she would be killed at once. She then made the little girl carry her load to Akpan's house.

When they arrived, Akpan was very much disappointed at the slave girl's appearance as she was not as pretty and fine as he had expected her to be. But as he had not seen Emme for seven years, he

105

had no suspicion that the girl was not really Emme for whom he had paid such a large dowry. He then called all his company together to play and feast, and when they arrived they were much astonished and said, "Is this the fine woman for whom you paid so much dowry and whom you told us so much about?" And Akpan could not answer them.

The slave girl was very cruel to Emme's little sister and wanted her to die so that her position would be more secure with her husband. She beat the little girl every day and always made her carry the largest water pot to the spring. She also made the child place her finger in the fire to use as firewood. During dinner, the slave girl went to the fire and got a hot piece of wood and burned the child all over the body with it. When Akpan asked her why she treated the child so badly, she replied that she was a slave that her father had bought for her.

One day, the little girl took the heavy water pot to the river to fill it but there was no one to lift it up for her. She remained a long time at the spring and at last began calling for her sister, Emme, to come and help her. Emme heard her little sister crying for her and begged the Water *Juju* to allow her to go and help her. He told her to go but that she must return to him again immediately. When the little girl saw her sister, she did not want to leave her and asked to be allowed to go into the hole with her. She told Emme how very badly she was being treated by the slave girl. Emme told her to patiently wait, that a day of vengeance would arrive sooner or later. The little girl went back to Akpan's house with a glad heart as she had seen her sister.

But when she got to the house, the slave girl asked why she took so long at the river. She then took a stick from the fire and burnt the little girl again very badly and starved her for the rest of the day. This went on for some time, until one day when the little girl went to the river for water again. After all the people had gone, she cried out for her sister as usual, but she did not come for a long time as there was a hunter from Akpan's town hiding and watching the hole and the Water *Juju* told Emme that she must not go. But as the little girl went on crying bitterly, Emme at last persuaded the *Juju* to let her go, promising to return quickly. When she emerged from the water, she looked very beautiful with the rays of the setting sun shining on her glistening body. She helped her little sister with her water pot and then disappeared into the hole again.

The hunter was amazed at what he had seen and when he returned, he told Akpan that a beautiful woman had come out of the water and had helped the little girl with her water pot. He also told Akpan that he was convinced that the girl he had seen at the spring was his proper wife, Emme, and that the Water *Juju* must have taken her. Akpan then made up his mind to go out and watch and see what happened. So in the early morning, the hunter came for him and they both went down to the river and hid in the forest near the water-hole.

When Akpan saw Emme come out of the water, he recognized her at once and went home and considered how he could get her out of the power of the Water *Juju*. He was advised by some of his friends to go to an old woman who frequently made sacrifices to the Water *Juju* and consult her as to what was the best thing to do. The old woman told him to bring one white slave, one white goat, one piece of white cloth, one white chicken, and a basket of eggs. Then when the great *Juju* day arrived, she would take them to the Water *Juju* and make a sacrifice of them on his behalf. She said the day after the sacrifice was made, the Water *Juju* would return the girl to her and she would bring her to Akpan.

Akpan bought the slave and took all the other things to the old woman, and when the day of the sacrifice arrived, he went with his friend, the hunter, to witness the old woman make the sacrifice. The slave was bound up and led to the hole, then the old woman called out to the Water *Juju* and cut the slave's throat with a sharp knife and pushed him into the hole. She then did the same to the goat and chicken, and also threw the eggs and cloth in on top of them.

After this had been done, they all returned to their homes. The next morning at dawn, the old woman went to the hole and found Emme standing at the side of the spring, so she told her that she was her friend and was going to take her to her husband. She then took Emme back to her own home, hid her in her room, and sent word to Akpan to come to her house and to take great care that the slave woman knew nothing about the matter. So Akpan left the house secretly by the back door and arrived at the old woman's house without meeting anybody.

When Emme saw Akpan, she asked for her little sister, so he sent his friend, the hunter, to the spring. He met her carrying her water pot to get the morning supply of water for the house and brought her to the old woman's house with him. After Emme had embraced her sister, she told her to return to the house and do something to annoy the slave woman, and then she was to run as fast as she could back to the old woman's house. They knew the slave girl would surely follow her and wanted her to meet them all inside the house and see Emme whom she believed she had killed.

The little girl did as she was told. Immediately she got into the house, she called out to the slave woman, "Do you know that you are a wicked woman and you have treated me very badly? I know you are only my sister's slave, and you will be properly punished." She then ran as hard as she could to the old woman's house. Immediately the slave woman heard what the little girl said, she was quite mad with rage and she seized a burning stick from the fire and ran after the child. But the little girl got to the house first and ran inside, the slave woman following close upon her heels with the burning stick in her hand. Emme came out and confronted the slave woman. She instantly recognized her mistress, whom she thought she had killed, so she stood quite still.

They all went back to Akpan's house and Akpan asked the slave woman what she meant by pretending that she was Emme, and why she had tried to kill her. But seeing she was found out, the slave woman had nothing to say. Many people were called to a feast to celebrate the recovery of Akpan's wife and when they had all come, he told them what the slave woman had done.

After this, Emme treated the slave girl in the same way as she had treated her little sister. She made her put her fingers in the fire, and burnt her with fire sticks. She also made her beat *foo-foo* with her head in a hollowed-out tree, and after a time she was tied up to a tree and starved to death. Ever since that time, when a man marries a girl, he is always present when she comes out of the fattening house and takes her home himself, so that such evil things as happened to Emme and her sister may not occur again.

ESSIDO AND HIS EVIL COMPANIONS

Chief Oborri lived in a town called Adiagor, which is on the right bank of the Calabar River. He was a wealthy chief and belonged to the *Ekpe* Society. He had many large canoes and a lot of slaves to paddle them. He used to fill up his canoes with new yams, with each canoe being under one head slave and containing eight paddles. The canoes were capable of holding three casks of palm-oil, and they cost eight hundred rods each. When they were full, about ten of them used to start off together and paddle to Rio del Rey. They went through creeks all the way, which run through mangrove swamps, with palm-oil trees here and there.

Sometimes in the tornado season, it was very dangerous crossing the creeks as the canoes were so heavily laden, having only a few inches above the water, that quite a small wave would fill the canoe and cause it to sink to the bottom. Although most of the boys could swim, it often happened that some of them were lost as there were many large alligators in these waters. After four days' hard paddling, they would arrive at Rio del Rey where they had very little difficulty in exchanging their new yams for bags of dried shrimps and sticks with smoked fish on them.

Chief Oborri had two sons named Eyo and Essido. Their mother died when they were babies so the children were brought up by their father. As they grew up, they developed entirely different characters. The eldest was very hardworking and led a solitary life but the younger son was fond of gaiety and was very lazy. In fact, he spent most of his time in the neighboring towns playing and dancing. When the two boys became 18 and 20 year olds respectively, their father died and they were left to look after themselves.

According to native custom, the elder son, Eyo, was entitled to the whole of his father's estate but being very fond of his younger brother, he gave him a large number of rods and some land with a house. Immediately Essido got the money, he became wilder than ever, gave big feasts to his companions and always had his house full of women on whom he spent large sums. Although the amount his brother had given him was very much, in the course of a few years, Essido had spent it all. He then sold his house and effects, and spent the proceeds on feasting.

While Essido was living this wasteful life, Eyo was working harder than ever at his father's old trade and had made many trips to

114

Rio del Rey himself. Almost every week, he had canoes laden with yams going down river and returning after about twelve days with shrimps and fishes which Eyo himself disposed of in the neighboring markets, and he rapidly became a very rich man. At intervals, he spoke harshly to Essido on his extravagance but his warnings had no effect; if anything, his brother became worse.

At last, the time arrived when all his money was spent, so Essido went to his brother and asked him to lend him two thousand rods. But Eyo refused and told Essido that he would not help him in any way to continue his present life of debauchery, but that if he liked to work on the farm and trade, he would give him a fair share of the profits. This, Essido indignantly refused, and went back to the town and consulted some of the very few friends he had left as to what was the best thing to do.

The men he spoke to were thoroughly bad men and had been living on Essido for a long time. They suggested to him that he should go round the town and borrow money from the people he had entertained, and then they would run away to Akpabryos town which was about four days' walk from Calabar. Essido did this and managed to borrow a lot of money, although many people refused to lend him anything. At night, he set off with his evil companions who carried his money, as they had not been able to borrow any themselves, being so well known. When they arrived at Akpabryos town, they found many beautiful women and graceful dancers. They started the same life again and after a few weeks most of the money had gone.

They then met and consulted together how to get more money. They advised Essido to return to his rich brother, pretend that he was going to work and give up his old life, and then get poison from a *Juju* man with which he would poison his brother's food and kill him. This way, Essido would inherit all his brother's wealth and they would be able to live the same way as they had. Essido, who had sunk very low, agreed to this plan and they left Akpabryos town the next morning.

After walking for two days, they arrived at a small hut in the bush where a man called Okponesip, an expert poisoner lived. He was the head *Juju* man of the country and when they had bribed him with eight hundred rods, he swore them to secrecy and gave Essido a small parcel containing a deadly poison which he said would kill his brother in three months. All he had to do was to place the poison in his brother's food.

When Essido returned to his brother's house he pretended to be very sorry about his former way of life and promised he was going to become responsible and hardworking. Eyo was very glad when he heard this and at once asked his brother in and gave him new clothes and so much to eat. In the evening, when supper was being prepared, Essido went into the kitchen, pretending he wanted to get a light from the fire for his pipe. The cook was absent and he could not see anyone about so he put the poison in the soup and returned to the living room. He then asked for some *tombo*, which was brought, and when he had finished it he said he did not want any supper and went to sleep. His brother, Eyo, had supper by himself and consumed all the soup. After a week, he began to feel very ill, and as the days passed he became worse, so he sent for his *Juju* man.

As soon as Essido saw him coming, he quietly left the house but the *Juju* man, by casting lots, discovered that it was Essido who had given poison to his brother. When he told Eyo this, he did not believe the *Juju* man and he sent him away. When Essido returned, his elder brother told him what the *Juju* man had said, but that he did not believe him for one moment and had sent him away. Essido was much relieved when he heard this but as he was anxious that no suspicion of the crime be attached to him, he went to the household *Juju* and having first sworn that he had never administered poison to his brother, he drank out of the pot.

Three months after he had taken the poison, Eyo died, much to the grief of everyone who knew him, as he was much respected not only on account of his great wealth but because he was also an upright and honest man who never did harm to anyone. Essido kept his brother's funeral according to the usual custom and there was much playing and dancing which was kept up for a long time. Then Essido paid off his old creditors in order to make himself popular, and kept open house, entertaining most lavishly and spending money in many foolish ways. All the bad women about gathered at his house and his old evil companions went on as they had done before.

Things got so bad that none of the respectable people would have anything to do with him. The chiefs, who were all friends of the late Eyo I., were very sad at his death. They knew that if he had not died he would have become a great and powerful chief. Eventually, when they saw the way Essido was squandering his late brother's estate, they came to the conclusion that he was a witch man and had poisoned his brother in order to acquire his wealth. So they made up their minds to give Essido the *Ekpawor Juju* for him to swear he didn't have a hand in his brother, Eyo I.'s death.

The *Ekpawor Juju* was a very strong medicine which gets into men's heads, so that when they have drunk it they are compelled to speak the truth and if they have done wrong they die very shortly. Essido was invited to a meeting at the conflict resolution house. When he arrived, the chiefs charged him with killing his brother through witchcraft. Essido denied having done so, but the chiefs told him that if he were innocent he must prove it by drinking the bowl of *Ekpawor* medicine which was placed before him. As he could not refuse, he drank the bowl off in great fear and trembling. Almost immediately, the *Juju* got hold of him and he confessed that he had poisoned his brother, but that his friends had advised him to do so. About two hours after drinking the *Ekpawor*, Essido died in great pain.

His friends were then brought to the meeting and tied up to posts and questioned as to the role they had played in the death of Eyo. As they were too frightened to answer, the chiefs told them that they knew from Essido that they had induced him to poison his brother. They were then taken to the place where Eyo was buried. The grave was dug open and their heads were cut off into the grave and their bodies were thrown in after them as a sacrifice for the wrong they had done. The grave was then filled up again. Ever since that time, whenever anyone is suspected of being a witch, he is tried by the *Ekpawor Juju*.

> **Comment [kC]:** Check if this is okay to replace "palaver house". Or use "*Ekpe* House".

119

THE DRUMMER
AND THE ALLIGATORS

There was once a woman named Affiong who lived at 'Nsidung, a small town to the south of Calabar. She was married to a chief of Hensham Town called Etim Ekeng. They had lived together for several years but had no children. The chief was very anxious to have a child during his lifetime and made sacrifices to his *Juju*, but they had no effect. So he went to a witch man who told him that the reason he had no children was that he was too rich. The chief then asked the witch man how he should spend his money in order to get a child, and he was told to make friends with everybody and give big feasts so that he could spend out of some of his money and become poor.

The chief went home and told his wife. The next day, his wife called all her friends and neighbors together and gave them a big dinner which cost a lot of money. Much food was consumed and large quantities of *tombo* were drunk. Then the chief entertained his friends too and that cost a lot more money. He also wasted a lot of money in the *Ekpe* house. When half of his property was wasted, his wife told him that she had conceived. The chief was very glad and he called a big feast for the next day.

In those days, all the rich chiefs of the country belonged to the Alligator cult and used to meet in the water. The reason they belonged to the cult was firstly, to protect their canoes when they went trading; and secondly, to destroy the canoes and property of the people who did not belong to their cult and to take their money and kill their slaves. Chief Etim Ekeng was a kind man and would not join this society, although he was repeatedly urged to do so.

After a time, a son was born to the chief and he called him Edet Etim. The chief then called the *Ekpe* society together and all the doors of the houses in the town were shut, the markets were stopped, and the women were not allowed to go outside their houses while the *Ekpe* was playing. This was kept up for several days and cost the chief a lot of money. Then he made up his mind that he would divide his property and give his son half when he became old enough. Unfortunately, three months after, the chief died and left his sorrowing wife to look after their little child.

The wife went into mourning for seven years for her husband, and after that time she became entitled to all his property, as the late chief had no brothers. She looked after the little boy very carefully until he grew up and became a very fine, healthy young man and was much admired by all the pretty girls in the town. But his mother warned him strongly not to go with them because they would make him become a bad man.

Whenever the girls had a play, they would invite Edet Etim. One day, he went to the play and they made him beat the drum for them to dance to. After much practice, he became the best drummer in the town and whenever the girls had a play they would call him to drum for them. A lot of the young girls left their husbands and went to Edet and asked him to marry them. This made all the young men of the town very jealous and when they met together at night, they considered what would be the best way to kill him. At last, they decided that when Edet went to bathe they would induce the alligators to take him.

One night, when he was washing, one alligator seized him by the foot and others came and seized him round the waist. He fought very hard but at last they dragged him into the deep water and took him to their home. When his mother heard this, she determined to do her best to recover her son, so she kept quiet until the morning. The young men saw that Edet's mother remained quiet and did not cry,

and they remembered the story of the hawk and the owl and determined to keep Edet alive for a few months.

At cockcrow, however, Edet's mother raised a cry and went to the grave of her dead husband in order to consult his spirit as to what she should do to recover her lost son. After a time, she went down to the beach with small young green branches in her hands with which she beat the water and called upon all the *Juju*s of the Calabar River to help her bring back her son. She then went home, got a load of rods and took them to a *Juju* man in the farm. His name was Ininen Okon. He was so called because he was very artful and had a great deal of strong *Juju*s.

The young boys all trembled with fear when they heard that Edet's mother had gone to Ininen Okon. They wanted to return Edet but could not as it was against the rules of their society. The *Juju* man having discovered that Edet was still alive and was being detained in the alligators' house, told the mother to be patient. After three days, Ininen himself joined another Alligators' Society and went to inspect the young alligators' house. He found a young man he knew who was left on guard when the alligators had gone to feed at the ebb of the tide. He came back and told the mother to wait so he could make a *Juju* which would cause them all to depart in seven days and leave no one in the house.

He made his *Juju* and one day, the young alligators said that as no one had come for Edet, they would all go at the ebb tide to feed and leave no one in charge of the house. When they returned they found Edet still there and everything as they had left it, as Ininen had not gone that day. Three days after, they all went away again and this time went a long way off, and did not return quickly.

. But Edet, having been in the water so long, was deaf and dumb. He then found several loin cloths which had been left behind by the young alligators, so he gathered them together and took them away to show to the king, and Ininen left the place, taking Edet with him.

He then called the mother to see her son, but when she came the boy could only look at her and could not speak. The mother embraced her boy but he took no notice, as he did not seem capable of understanding anything, but sat down quietly. Then the *Juju* man told Edet's mother that he would cure her son in a few days, so he made several *Juju*s and gave Edet medicine, and after a time the boy recovered his speech and became sensible again.

Then Edet's mother put on a mourning cloth and pretended that her son was dead, and did not tell the people he had come back to her. When the young alligators returned, they found that Edet was gone and that someone had taken their loin cloths. They were therefore afraid and made inquiries if Edet had been seen, but they could hear nothing about him as he was hidden in a farm and his mother continued to wear her mourning cloth in order to deceive them.

Nothing happened for six months and they had quite forgotten all about the matter. Affiong, Edet's mother, then went to the chiefs of the town and asked them to hold a large meeting of all the people, both young and old, at the *Ekpe* house so that her late husband's property might be divided up in accordance with the native custom, as her son had been killed by the alligators.

The next day, the chiefs called all the people together. Affiong had then taken her son to a small room at the back of the *Ekpe* house and left him there with the seven loin cloths which the *Juju* man took from the alligators' home. When the chiefs and all the people were seated, Affiong stood up and addressed them, saying, "Chiefs and young men of my town, eight years ago my husband was a fine young man. He married me and we lived together for many years without having any children. At last I had a son, but my husband died a few months afterwards. I brought up my boy carefully, but as he was a good drummer and dancer, the young men were jealous and had him caught by the alligators. Is there anyone present who can tell me what my son would have become if he had lived?" She then asked them what they thought of the alligator society which had killed so many young men.

The chiefs, who had lost a lot of slaves, told her that if she could produce evidence against any member of the society they would destroy it at once. She then called upon Ininen to appear with her son, Edet. He came out from the room, leading Edet by the hand and placed the bundle of loin cloths before the chiefs. The young men were very much surprised when they saw Edet and wanted to leave the *Ekpe* house. But the chiefs ordered them to sit down at once or they would receive three hundred lashes of the whip. They sat down and the *Juju* man explained how he had gone to the alligators' home and had brought Edet back to his mother. He also said that he had found the seven loin cloths in the house but did not wish to say anything about them, as the owners of some of the cloths were sons of the chiefs.

The chiefs, who were anxious to stop the bad society, told him, however, to speak at once and tell them everything. Then he undid the bundle and took the cloths out one by one, at the same time calling upon the owners to come and take them. When they came to take their clothes, they were told to remain where they were and to name their company. The seven young men then gave the names of all the members of their society, thirty-two in all. These men were all placed in a line, and the chiefs passed a sentence which was that they should all be killed the next morning on the beach. They were all tied together to posts and seven men were placed as a guard over them. They made fires and beat drums all the night.

Early in the morning, at about 4 a.m., the big wooden drum was placed on the roof of the *Ekpe* house and was beaten to celebrate the death of the evildoers, which was the custom in those days. The boys were then unfastened from the posts, had their hands tied behind their backs, and were marched down to the beach. When they arrived there, the head chief stood up and addressed the people. "This is a small town of which I am chief, and I am determined to stop this bad custom as so many men have been killed." He then told a man who had a sharp machete to cut off one man's head. He then told another man who had a sharp knife to skin another young man alive. A third man who had a heavy stick was ordered to beat another to death, and so the chief went on and killed all the thirty-two young men in the most horrible ways he could think of. Some of them were tied to posts in the river and left there until the tide came up and drowned them. Others were flogged to death.

After they had all been killed, no one was killed by alligators for many years. But after a while, the land on the road between the beach and the town fell in, making a very large and deep hole which was said to be the home of the alligators. The people have ever since tried to fill it up but have not been able to do so.

THE 'NSASAK BIRD
AND THE ODUDU BIRD

A long time ago, in the days of King Afam of Calabar, the king wanted to know if there was any animal or bird which was capable of enduring hunger for a long period. When he found one, the king said, he would make him a chief of his tribe. The 'Nsasak bird was very small, having a shining breast of green and red. He also had blue and yellow feathers and red round the neck, and his chief food consisted of ripe palm nuts. The Odudu bird, in contrast, was much larger, about the size of a magpie, with a great deal of feathers but a very thin body. He had a long tail and his coloring was black and brown with a cream-colored breast. He lived chiefly on grasshoppers, and was very fond of crickets which make a noise at night.

The 'Nsasak bird and the Odudu were great friends and used to live together. They both made up their minds that they would go before the king and try to be made chiefs, but the Odudu bird was quite confident that he would win as he was so much bigger than the 'Nsasak bird. He therefore offered to starve for seven days. The king then told them to build houses which he would inspect, and then he would have them locked up and the one who could remain the longest without eating would be made the chief.

They both then built their houses but the 'Nsasak bird, who was very cunning, thought that he could not possibly live for seven days without eating anything. He therefore made a tiny hole in the wall (being very small himself), and covered it up so that the king would not notice it on his inspection. The king came and looked carefully over both houses but failed to detect the little hole in the 'Nsasak bird's house, as it had been hidden so carefully. He therefore declared that both houses were safe and then ordered the two birds to go inside their respective houses, and the doors were carefully fastened on the outside.

Every morning at dawn, the 'Nsasak bird would escape through the small opening he had left high up in the wall, fly away a long distance and enjoy himself all day, taking care, however, that none of the people on the farms should see him. Then when the sun went down, he would fly back to his little house and creep through the hole in the wall, closing it carefully after him. When he was safely inside, he would call out to his friend, the Odudu, and ask him if he felt hungry; and tell him that he must bear it well if he wanted to win, as he, the 'Nsasak bird, was very fit, and could go on for a long time.

For several days this went on, the voice of the Odudu bird growing weaker every night, until at last he could no longer reply. Then the little bird knew that his friend must be dead. He was very sorry but could not report the matter, as he was supposed to be confined inside his house. When the seven days had expired, the king came and had the doors of the houses opened. The 'Nsasak bird at once flew out, and perching on the branch of a tree which grew near, sang most merrily. But the Odudu bird was found to be dead and there was very little left of him as the ants had eaten most of his body, leaving only the feathers and bones on the floor. The king therefore at once appointed the 'Nsasak bird to be the head chief of all the small birds.

In Ibibio, even to the present time, the small boys who have bows and arrows are presented with a prize which sometimes takes the shape of a female goat if they manage to shoot an 'Nsasak bird. The 'Nsasak bird is the king of the small birds, and most difficult to shoot on account of his wiliness and his small size.

THE ELECTION
OF THE KING BIRD

Old Town, Calabar, once had a king called Essiya, who, like most of the Calabar kings in the olden days, was rich and powerful. But although he was so wealthy, he did not possess many slaves. He therefore used to call upon the animals and birds to help his people with their work. In order to get the work done quickly and well, he decided to appoint head chiefs of all the different species. The elephant, he appointed king of the beasts of the forest, and the hippopotamus, king of the water animals, until at last it came to the turn of the birds to have their king elected.

Essiya thought for some time which would be the best way to make a good choice but could not make up his mind as there were so many different birds who all considered they had claims. There was the hawk with his swift flight, and of hawks there were several species. There were the herons to be considered, and the big spur-winged geese, the hornbill or toucan tribe; and the game birds such as guinea-fowl, the partridge, and the bustards. Then again, of course, there were all the big crane tribe, who walked about the sandbanks in the dry season, but disappeared when the river rose, and the big black-and-white fishing eagles.

When the king thought of the plover tribe, the sea-birds, including the pelicans, the doves, and the numerous shy birds who live in the forest, all of whom sent in claims, he got so confused that he decided to have a trial by ordeal of combat. He sent word round the whole country for all the birds to meet the next day and fight it out between themselves, and that the winner would be known as the "king bird" ever afterwards.

The following morning, many thousands of birds came and there was much screeching and flapping of wings. The hawk tribe soon drove all the small birds away and harassed the big waders so much that they very shortly disappeared, followed by the geese who made much noise and winged away in a straight line as if they were playing "Follow my leader". The big forest birds who liked to lead a secluded life very soon got tired of all the noise and bustle, and after a few croaks and other weird noises, went home.

The game birds had no chance and hid in the bush, so that very soon the only birds left were the hawks and the big black-and-white fishing eagle who was perched on a tree, calmly watching everything. The scavenger hawks were too fat and lazy to take much interest in what went on, and were quietly ignored by the fighting tribe who were very busy circling and swooping on one another with much whistling going on. Higher and higher they went, until they disappeared out of sight. Then a few would return to earth, some of them badly torn and with many feathers missing.

At last the fishing eagle said, "When you have quite finished with this foolishness please tell me, and if any of you fancy yourselves at all, come to me and I will settle your chances of being elected head chief once and for all." But when they saw his terrible beak and cruel claws and knowing his great strength and ferocity, they stopped fighting between themselves and acknowledged the fishing eagle to be their master. Essiya then declared that Ituen, which was the name of the fishing eagle, was the head chief of all the birds, and should from that day be known as the "king bird".

From that time to the present day, whenever the young men of the country go to fight, they always wear three of the long black-and-white feathers of the king bird in their hair, one on each side and one in the middle, as they are believed to impart much courage and skill to the wearer. If a young man is not possessed of any of these feathers when he goes out to fight, he is looked upon as a very small boy indeed.

THE END

NOTES

- A piece of cloth is generally about 8 yards long by 1 yard broad, and is valued at 5s.

- A rod is made of brass, and is worth 3d. It is in the shape of a narrow croquet hoop, about 16 inches long and 6 inches across. A rod is native currency in Cross River.

- The Fattening House is a room where a girl is kept for some weeks before her marriage. She is given a so much food and made as fat as possible because fatness is considered a great beauty by the Efik people.

- The Ekpe Society has many branches, extending from Calabar up the Cross River, as far as Cameroun. Formerly, this society used to levy blackmail to a certain extent and collect debts for people. The head *Juju*, or fetish man, of each society is disguised and frequently wears a hideous mask. There is a bell tied round his waist, hanging behind and concealed by feathers; this bell makes a noise as he runs. When the *Ekpe* is out, women are not allowed outside their houses, and even at the present time the women pretend to be very frightened. The *Ekpe* very often carries a whip in his hand, and hits out blindly at anyone he comes across. He runs round the town, followed by young men of his society beating drums and firing off guns. There is generally much drinking going on when the *Ekpe* is playing. There is an *Ekpe* House in most towns, the end part of which is screened off for the *Ekpe* to change in. Inside the house are hung human skulls and the skulls of buffalo or bush cows (as they are called); also heads of the various antelopes, crocodiles, apes, and other animals which have been killed by the members. The skulls of cows and goats killed by the society are also hung up. A fire is always kept in the *Ekpe* house, and in the morning and late afternoon, the members of the society frequently meet there to drink gin and palm wine.

- *Foo-foo*: Yams boiled and mashed up.

- *Tombo* is an intoxicating drink made from the juice extracted from the *tombo* palm, and which ferments very quickly. It is drawn from the tree twice a day - in the morning very early, and again in the afternoon.

- Machete is a long sharp knife in general use throughout the country. It has a wooden handle and is about two feet six inches long and two inches wide.

- The *Esere* or Calabar bean is a strong poison and was formerly much used by the natives. These beans are ground up in a stone mortar and are then swallowed by the accused person. If the man dies he is considered guilty, but if he lives he is supposed to have proved his innocence of the charge brought against him. Death generally ensues about two hours after the poison is administered. If the accused takes a sufficient amount of the ground-up beans to make him vomit, it will probably save his life; otherwise he will die in great pain.

- A stick of fish consisted of two sticks with a big fish in the middle of each and small fish at each end, there being eight fish on each stick, making sixteen in all. These sticks were then tied together and smoked over wood fires until they were quite dried. One stick of fish would sell at Calabar in the dry season time for between 3s. 6d. to 5s. A stick would be got for five large yams which cost Chief Oborri only 1s., so a large profit was made on each canoe load - the canoes carrying about a thousand yams each. A bag of shrimps would be bartered for twenty-five large yams and the shrimps would be sold for 15s., being a profit of 10s. on each bag. At the present time however, the same sized bag of shrimps in the wet season would sell at Calabar for £3, 10s., and in the dry season for between £1, 10s. and £2.

- *Juju* : Every compound has a small *Juju* in the center which are generally a few curiously shaped stones and a small tree on which the *Nsiat* bird often builds. There is sometimes a species of cactus at the foot, an earthenware pot is supported on sticks against the tree and tied on with *tie-tie* or native rope. In this pot there is always a very foul-smelling liquid with some rotten eggs floating in it. Small sacrifices of chickens are made to these *Juju's* to regularly appeal to them. The liquid is sometimes taken as a specific remedy against sickness or poison. In the dry season, the author has often observed large spiders with their webs all over these *Juju's* but they are never touched. There is also a roughly carved image of wood and sometimes an old machete and some broken earthenware on the ground, with a brass rod or manila. It is generally a very dirty spot.

- King bird: As the king bird is always very difficult to shoot with a bow and arrow owing to his sharp and keen sight, when young men want his feathers, they set traps for him baited with rats, which catch him by the foot in a noose when he seizes them. Except when they are nesting, king birds roost on very high trees, sometimes as many as twenty or thirty on neighboring trees. They fly many miles from where they get their food and arrive at their roosting place just before the sun sets, leaving the next morning at dawn for their favorite haunts. They are very regular in their habits and you can see them every night at the same time, coming from the same direction and flying over the same trees, generally fairly high up in the air. There is a strong belief amongst many natives on the Cross River that the king bird has the power of influencing the luck (or otherwise) of a canoe. For example, when a trader, having bought a new canoe, is going to market and a king bird crosses the river from right to left, then if he is unlucky at the market that day, whenever the king bird again crosses that particular canoe from right to left he will be unlucky and the bad luck will stick to the canoe. If, in contrast, the bird for the first time crosses from left to right, and he is fortunate in his dealings that day at the market, then he will always be lucky in that canoe the day he sees a king bird flying across the river from the left to the right-hand side.